by Michael Eidam

This is a work of fiction. Characters in this novel are either the product of the author's imagination or are used fictitiously without any intent to describe their actual conduct. Furthermore, no opinions in this book should be taken seriously—especially the one about mustard. Mustard has its place in the world—at the very least on a hot dog if not on a hamburger—and can actually be quite tasty when spicy brown.

Cover illustration by Dago Baute.

For Jackson, Carter, and Campbell, who wanted a story about dragons. At least, when I started this book they wanted a story about dragons. If that's no longer true, it's not my fault for taking too long to write it; it's their fault for growing up.

1

Dragon Fruit

Slide, thrust, jump, slash!

Carter threw open the front door, tossed his backpack onto the bench in the entranceway, and sprinted upstairs to the game room. On the bus ride home, he had figured out how to defeat the Red Dragon in Dragonsbane: *Slide, thrust, jump, slash!* He raced against his memory, afraid he might forget the move before he could try it.

He turned on the game console and the Dance Party game came onscreen. Carter grunted. Of course his sister had been playing Dance Party. But his annoyance turned to panic when he realized he was powerless to change the game—the controllers were missing! He searched the TV console in a frenzy, sweeping game cases off the shelves, but came up empty. *Maybe they're on the couch.* He turned, and only then realized his little sister was sitting on the couch watching him. She wore the look of someone who was up to no good: a smirk dotted with eager eyes.

"Where are the controllers?" Carter demanded.

"I dunno," she replied. "Maybe Mom took them."

"Why would Mom take them?"

"I dunno. Maybe she thinks you're playing too much Dragonsbane."

Carter's eyes narrowed. "Campbell. Where are they?"

"I don't know," she said innocently. "But I can probably find them."

"*Find* them? You *hid* them."

"No I didn't," she shot back. Then she softened back into her sweet voice. "Do you want me to look for them?"

Carter grunted in frustration.

She took that as a yes. "Okay, but if I find them, then I want to play Dance Party."

"Dance Party is so lame."

Campbell gasped. "Carter, that's a bad word." And then a smile snuck onto her face as she waited for Carter to understand the threat: she would tell Mom what he said.

"Fine," he relented. "I'll play *one* game. But then I get to play Dragonsbane. I figured out how to defeat the Red Dragon." *Slide, thrust, jump, slash,* he reminded himself.

Campbell ran out of the room and came back seconds later with the two game controllers. "I found them."

Carter rolled his eyes. She was fooling no one. But if he fought with her about it, he would just get in trouble, probably get punished, and not be able to try his new move on the Red Dragon. He needed to keep his eyes on the prize and play nice.

Campbell launched the Dance Party game and shimmied her shoulders to the intro music as she navigated the game's menu. "I'm going to be Glo," she said as she selected her character—a punky-looking girl with spiky blonde hair and a bright pink jumpsuit with light blue racing stripes. "Pick your character, Carter."

"Carter pressed the button without even changing the character, so he ended up selecting a woman with short black hair wearing a black tank top and black leggings.

"Ooh. Good choice, Carter."

"Whatever."

"Okay, get ready . . ."

The dance music started, and Campbell began to move along with her character on the screen—shaking her hips, dipping her shoulders, twirling her arms in the air. Every time she executed a successful dance move a computerized voice would shout a supportive message like "Wow!" "Good job!" "Way to go!" and the words would flash onscreen.

By contrast, Carter just stood there, barely moving, with a scowl on his face, waiting for the torture to end. The game tried to encourage him with messages like "Come on!" and "You can do it!" but they had no effect. He didn't *want* to do it. He *wanted* to play Dragonsbane. *Slide, thrust, jump, slash!*

"I'm beating you, Carter," Campbell said with a laugh. She was beaming with joy.

"Whatever," he said.

The game finished and an explosion of congratulatory lights burst around Campbell's character. "I won!" she cheered. "Good game, Carter," she added after a long breath.

"Now I get to play Dragonsbane," he said, holding out his hand for the main controller.

"No, I won. The person who wins gets to decide what we do next."

"That is *not* what we said."

"It's my decision and I say we play Dance Party again," Campbell said as she restarted the game.

With the stakes redefined, Carter took the second game a lot more seriously and the frequent calls of "Wow!" "Good job!" "Now you got it!" coming from his side of the screen quickly turned Campbell's joy into nervousness. She glanced over and saw Carter was up by almost a hundred points with only a few seconds to go. And then, in a blink of an eye, the 'Quit Game' menu popped onscreen and the game was over.

"Oops," Campbell said. "I guess we need to start over."

"You did that on purpose!"

"I didn't do it."

"I won. I get to play Dragonsbane now." He threw out his hand, demanding the controller.

"You didn't win! The game ended before we finished. So, I still get to decide what we do, and I say we play Tea Party."

"I am *not* playing Tea Party!"

Carter should have seen this coming. Campbell was never satisfied with Dance Party—it only *started* with Dance Party. Her real objective was to get him to play dolls, or worse, Tea Party. Playing dolls wasn't so bad, at least he could make them fight like action figures. But Tea Party was the worst! You just sat around with her stuffed animals and pretended to drink tea. He was in no mood for that nonsense.

"I won! Now, give me the controller!" Carter grabbed the main controller, but Campbell held on and stepped back, trying to pull it free.

"All I have to do is cry and you'll get in trouble," she warned.

"I don't care," he said and ripped the controller out of her hands.

Campbell erupted into a screaming cry: "Mom! Carter hurt me!"

Carter knew the routine. He knew what was coming next. Their mom entered the room and surveyed the situation. Campbell was crying and Carter was within arm's reach of her. That was all she needed to see.

"Carter?! What did you do?"

"I didn't do anything?"

"He hurt me!" Campbell screamed, before whining as if suffering the most intense pain imaginable.

"I didn't even touch her!"

"Then why is she crying?"

"Because she's a brat!"

"Carter!"

"I am not a brat!" Campbell yelled. She erupted in tears that seemed a lot more sincere than the ones she was crying earlier and ran out of the room.

"Carter, she just wants to play with you," his mother said.

"No, she doesn't. She just wants to cry and get me in trouble. I wish she was never born!"

"That's enough! Go to your room!"

Carter didn't argue, at least not with words. But he frowned with every muscle in his face, stomped to his bedroom, and slammed his door in protest.

***

Carter lay on his bed and stared at the ceiling, thinking about everything in life that was unfair: his mom, his sister, fourth grade, the third level of Dragonsbane.

Slide, slash, jump, thrust. Or was it slide, thrust, jump, slash? Ah, man!!

His thoughts were interrupted by the sound of his father coming home. He had been in China on business for the past week, and a long trip usually meant a present.

Carter rushed downstairs. He rounded the corner into the kitchen just as his father placed a small bag on the counter next to a wooden box. Campbell and his older brother, Jackson, were already there.

"Dad?!" he shouted.

"Hey, Carter!"

Carter ran to his father and gave him a big hug. "What's in the bag?" he asked.

"Would you believe me if I told you it was a dragon?"

Carter watched with wide eyes as his father pulled a wad of paper out of the bag. He slowly unraveled it to reveal a small dragon stature.

"Whoa! Cool!"

His father pulled out another wad of paper and unraveled a dragon statue for Jackson.

"Cool! Thanks, Dad."

"Dragons are annoying," Campbell said.

Carter rolled his eyes. 'Annoying' was Campbell's new favorite word. Anything she didn't like had one day, out of nowhere, become annoying.

"Well, then I guess it's a good thing I didn't get you a dragon," her father replied.

"You didn't?!" she whined.

"Nope." He smiled and pulled a small stuffed panda bear out of the bag.

Campbell's face beamed. "I *love* panda bears!"

"I know."

She hugged it tight, sighed happily, and hugged it again. But then her eyes gravitated toward Carter's statue. "Carter, can I see your dragon?"

She reached out a hand to take it from him, but he turned to block her grasp with his shoulder. "No," he said. "Gees, I just got it."

"Carter, let your sister see it," his mother said.

"Here, Campbell, you can see mine." Jackson handed her his statue and turned his attention to the wooden box, eyeing the exotic drawings on its lid. *Or is that writing?* "What's in the box?" he asked.

"Ah," their father answered, smiling with excited eyes. He pulled the box closer and undid the two latches on the front that kept the lid locked down. He paused before lifting it. "Every morning at breakfast the hotel served the most delicious fruit—something I had never eaten before. Guess what it's called?"

The kids just shrugged.

"Dragon fruit." He slowly opened the crate as if there was a magical treasure inside. But instead, resting on plush red fabric, were three of the weirdest-looking things the kids had ever seen.

"They look like alien eggs," Carter said.

"They look gross," Campbell added.

"Maybe," their father said. "But they taste delicious. I was in a street market shopping for your presents when I came upon a vendor selling these. He said this type of dragon fruit was extremely rare and could only be found in a remote part of China. These were his last three."

Their father took one out of the crate and began cutting it into pieces as he continued his story. "I asked him how it was different than what they served in the hotel and he said, 'Because these are *magical.*'"

"Magical?" Carter repeated with wide eyes.

Their father laughed. "Well, between my rusty Chinese and his desire to make a sale, the more reliable translation is probably 'delicious.' He asked me if I had any children and when I told him I did, he said I had to buy them for you. He made me promise not to eat any of it and save it all for you."

"Why?"

"He said it wouldn't work for adults, not pure enough or something like that." Their father laughed as he continued the tale. "At least that's what I *think* he said. I didn't understand half of what he told me. He went on and on about how you had to plant the seeds to grow a new tree in case you needed to go back."

"Go back where?"

"China, I guess. Who knows? He shattered all confidence I had in my ability to speak Chinese."

The kids gathered around to get a better look at the fruit. Inside, it was white with tiny black seeds. But it wasn't a plain white, Carter noticed. The white seemed to shine, and the seeds looked like tiny polished jewels.

"Who wants to try some?" their father asked.

"I'll try it." Jackson said. His father handed him one of the cut-up pieces. The others waited for Jackson's verdict. He plopped it into his mouth and his eyes popped wide with surprise. "Wow, that is *so* good!" he said.

"I want to try!"

"Me too!"

Their father divvied up equal shares, saving a piece for their mother. *One piece can't hurt.*

She took a small bite: "Ew, it's too sour."

"It's sweet," Carter said.

"Like watermelon—only sweeter," Jackson added.

"Like candy," Campbell said.

"You kids are nuts," their mother replied. She spit it out in the sink and washed out her mouth.

"I guess that street merchant was telling the truth," their father said as he watched the kids gobble it all down.

***

Jackson and Carter put their new dragon statues on the nightstand between their twin beds, and then crawled under their covers. Their father was tucking Carter into bed when Campbell entered the boys' room dragging a small mattress behind her. She dropped it on the floor and pushed it against the wall opposite the end of their beds.

"Ah, man!" Carter said.

"Dad," Jackson added plaintively.

Campbell liked to sleep in their room, which didn't used to be an issue. But lately, she had been having nightmares and begun sleepwalking. She would wake up in the middle of the night screaming which would wake Jackson and Carter up. One time, she sleepwalked out of the room, and when Jackson tried to wake her, she sleep-smacked him in the face! He preferred a good night's sleep to a midnight face-smacking.

Campbell eyed her father intently, waiting for his verdict. She used to sleep in their room all the time, but lately they had been so mean to her. If they had a game the next day or a test in school, they would use it as an excuse to kick her out. Especially Carter. He was such a smelly pants.

"It's okay, boys," their father said in a tone that conveyed, *Don't be mean to your sister*. And with that, Campbell ran back to her room to get her pillow and blanket.

Once she was gone, their father sat on Carter's bed. "Your mother told me what you said about Campbell today."

"Dad—"

"You boys need to be nicer to your sister. She looks up to you. You're her older brothers, you need to look out for her. Protect her."

She needs to be nicer to me*!* Carter thought, but he knew there was no point arguing. So he turned away and buried his face in his pillow.

Campbell reentered with her pillow and blanket, as well as her new stuffed panda bear. She laid down on the mattress, and hugged her stuffed bear tight as her father tucked her in. "I like hugs," the panda bear said to her surprise, and she hugged it again.

"Good night kids," their father said as he turned off their bedroom light.

Jackson snuggled up and watched his new dragon statue disappear in the darkness. He closed his eyes and quickly fell asleep.

***

What is that smell? Jackson wondered. Whatever it was, it was strong enough to wake him up. It smelled like a barbeque pit—part burning wood, part burning rock. He cracked open his eyes to see if it was still nighttime outside, but his bedroom window wasn't there. His entire *bedroom* wasn't there. He sat up in a panic to find he was outside sitting on black, gravelly sand. The air was hazy like a morning mist, only hot and muggy instead of cool and crisp. He could feel the weight of it on his face. The sky was painted red and orange as if the air itself was on fire. In the dim light, through the haze, he saw dark, scary-looking shapes all around him. They looked like monstrous claws reaching out of the ground.

Where am I? he wondered.

2

Dragon Dreams

Last summer, wildfires raged in the hills a few miles from Jackson's home. The fires were huge and colored the sky dark brown and orange. When he went outside that morning, the air was heavy with smoke and heat and there was black soot all over the ground. Ashes fell from the sky like black snowflakes. It was hard to breathe. It was also eerily quiet. Birds and other animals—other people—were nowhere to be seen or heard. It was like being on another planet, like Mars or something.

This place reminded him of that.

How did I get here? he wondered. He looked over and noticed Carter was lying a few feet away—where his bed would have been if they were still in their room.

"Carter," he whispered.

Carter grumbled.

"Carter!" Jackson said again—this time with more bark than whisper.

"Wha—*ut*!" Carter rolled over as if he had every intention of ignoring Jackson and going back to sleep, when his face scraped against the gravelly sand. He popped his head up and looked at the ground in confusion. "What the heck?" He bolted to his feet and wiped away a few chunks of gravel that had stuck to his cheek.

Jackson saw Campbell was there too, cuddling with her panda bear. He gently shook her shoulder. "Campbell, wake up," he whispered.

She stretched and yawned, but then coughed when the foul taste of the air touched her tongue. She looked around at their strange surroundings with growing panic. "Where are we?" she asked.

"I don't know," Jackson said as he helped Campbell to her feet.

"What's that noise?" Carter wondered. A distant rumble crawled towards them out of the silence.

Jackson turned toward the noise and saw dark clouds gathering in the sky beyond the tree line. The sounds grew louder and more violent. The wind picked up and threw itself against the trees like it was attacking them. The tree branches swung wildly as if they were trying to fight back.

"Let's go check it out," Jackson said.

They left the clearing and headed down a thin path that cut through the jungle. The ground looked like volcanic rock and yet trees and plants grew all around. Jackson paused to examine one of the trees. It only had two branches that extended from the trunk halfway up the tree. From each branch grew one giant leaf. What should have been tree bark looked more like scales. The kind of scales you would find on a—

Jackson heard a whoosh behind him, and he turned to see a charred dragonfly with a trail of smoke falling toward the ground. A nearby plant opened its snout-like mouth and a long, forked tongue whipped out and snatched the dragonfly from midair. The plant chomped the bug in its teeth—large, sharp teeth, like the kind you would find on a—

Dragon, Jackson thought. He looked back up at the tree, and what before looked like two branches with large leaves, now looked more like wings. Dragon's wings. The branches looked more like muscular arms and toward their ends, they fingered off into smaller branches that resembled claws.

Jackson ran his fingers along the scaly-looking tree trunk when he heard:

"Ow! Mom, Carter bit me!"

"I didn't touch you!"

"I'm bleeding!" Campbell screamed.

Jackson rushed to catch up and found his brother and sister surrounded by the same dragon-like plants.

Campbell was inspecting the bite on her arm while behind her a plant licked blood from its teeth. It leaned toward her with opened jaws. It was about to dig its teeth into her leg when Jackson ran over and kicked it away. The dragon plant growled and spat fire at them. Jackson grabbed Campbell and pulled her away just as the flame shot past them. All the nearby plants growled and barked at them like wild beasts.

"What the—?!" Carter said, mystified. He turned to Campbell, "I told you it wasn't me."

Campbell was dumbfounded. She looked at the bite on her arm, then back at the plant, and then screamed, "Mom! That plant bit me!"

Jackson eyed the surrounding plants, trying to gauge if they would attack. They were all leaning toward them with open mouths, barking mad. "Let's get out of here," he said.

They raced down the path to where it ended at the edge of a cliff overlooking a huge canyon. A storm was visible on the horizon. The wind howled, and dark clouds swept over the land.

Now where do we go? Jackson thought.

"That cloud looks like a dragon," Carter said, pointing toward the distant sky.

Jackson nodded. It was not a faint resemblance, like if you looked closely enough you could kind of see a dragon shape in the cloud. It *really* looked like a dragon!

Off in the distance, the sea raged and its waves pounded against the sheer rock cliffs that lined the water. It almost looked as if the waves were charging against the cliffs, trying to knock them down. A large section of rock broke away and crashed into the sea.

An eruption of lava and rock spewed out of the ocean, followed by another and then another running in a line fifty yards from the cliffs. As the debris settled back into the sea, it created a long barrier island that prevented the waves from reaching the cliffs.

A river cut through the center of the canyon, but instead of leading out to sea, it looked as if the river originated from the sea and flowed inland. Water overflowed its banks as if the river was trying to drown the entire valley.

The ground quaked and rocks from the nearby cliffs broke free and tumbled down into the river, creating a bridge across the water.

A stampede of creatures shot out from the corner of the canyon, dust exploding into the air behind them. They raced across the bridge and charged toward the mountains at the far end of the valley. As the creatures crossed the river, a wave swept across the rock bridge and knocked two of them into the water. It carried them downstream toward the ocean.

The stampede raced on only to be met by a furious wind that howled throughout the canyon. The wind was trying to blow the creatures back, but the stampede continued on through the onslaught. The creatures were about to climb a mountain when a lightning bolt shot out from the clouds and struck the mountaintop. It exploded into thousands of rocks that went tumbling down toward the creatures below.

Then the same mountain erupted, throwing a blast of fiery rock and smoke into the air that cut through the clouds and sent them scattering. The stampede continued its way up the mountain slope.

Thunder roared and huge hailstones dropped through the smokey sky and pounded the animals as they charged up the mountain.

A chorus of screeches rang out. "Look!" Carter yelled as flying creatures swooped down from the clouds.

"Are those birds?" Campbell asked.

"They don't sound like birds," Jackson said.

"They're as big as the other animals," Carter added. "They must be huge!"

The sky creatures joined forces with the fierce winds and charged into the stampede. Several creatures tumbled down the mountain.

The volcano erupted again sending more fire-blazed rocks into the air. A lava rock struck one of the sky creatures and it screamed in pain and crashed to the ground.

The sky grew darker. More thunder cracked, more lighting flashed, and more hailstones pounded the ground like small artillery fire. The kids watched in stunned silence, totally unaware that a group of dark clouds was floating their way!

A bolt of lightning shot out and struck a nearby tree. The tree screamed! There was no other way to describe the sound: the tree actually *screamed* in pain.

"Come on," Jackson said, "We need to find cover." He turned and led the others away from the storm. They raced along the path that cut through the jungle when something crashed to the ground in front of them, blocking their way. They couldn't see what it was at first because it crashed with such force it sent a giant cloud of black sand into the air that hid everything from view. They coughed and waved the dirty air from their faces.

As the dust slowly settled, it revealed a large creature standing before them. It had a smooth, pure-white belly and its back was covered in off-white scales. The scales seemed to shine like pearls. From its back sprang two giant wings. Steam rose from its snout, and its eyes sparkled like diamonds.

"A dragon," Carter said with wonder. He seemed more amazed than scared.

There was a long, tense moment as the dragon looked from one kid to the other, taking them all in with its sparkling silver eyes, unsure what to make of them. Then it let out a howling roar that sounded—and felt—like storm winds blowing in their faces. Campbell screamed and took off running in the opposite direction. The dragon darted after her, knocking the boys to the ground as it flew by.

Carter rolled over just in time to see the dragon grab Campbell in its claws and fly off into the air.

Jackson was already on his feet running after her. "Campbell!" he yelled as the dragon flew off into the distance.

The boys made it to the cliff and watched in horror as the dragon carried Campbell off into the center of the storm. She disappeared into the dark clouds, lightning flashing all around her, screaming, "Jackson!"

The boys were frozen in disbelief. Carter shook his head. "Mom's going to blame me for this, I just know it."

A heavy thumping sound climbed up from below the cliff, and before they even had a chance to wonder what it was, a dragon drifted up in front of them. It let out a tremendous howl that sent their ears ringing, their hair flying, and their noses twitching. *Man, dragons have terrible breath*, Carter thought.

"Come on!" Jackson yelled. They turned and sprinted back the other way. As they ran through the jungle, they heard the dragon flying overhead. Another howl filled their ears, followed by the whoompff, whoompff, whoompff of large flapping wings. Jackson looked up. The dragon was following them, soaring above the tree line and eyeing them intently, waiting for the right moment to strike.

The boys continued running as fast as they could, not sure where to go, where to hide. Carter could see the dragon's shadow covering the ground around him. The path they were on widened and then the dragon's shadow began to grow— it was swooping down toward them. It howled with fury!

"Duck," Jackson yelled as he grabbed Carter and pulled him to the ground. A foul wind blew over them as the dragon swept by, just barely missing them with its giant claws. It soared into a turn, and then headed back toward them. Jackson thought they were done for, but as the dragon descended, a nearby tree reached out with its wing-like branch and swatted the dragon to the ground. The disoriented dragon shook its head, trying to regain its senses. It looked up at the tree and roared.

"Come on!" Jackson shouted. He pulled Carter to his feet and they burst out into the clearing and then turned down another path.

Carter looked back to see the dragon leap after them, but the nearby tree leaned over and grabbed the dragon out of the air with its claw-like branches.

"Jackson, look!"

The boys stopped to watch as the tree pulled the dragon tight against its trunk and wrapped it in its giant leaves until only the dragon's head was visible. All of the nearby plants barked in fury at the captured dragon.

The ground shook as something large charged through the jungle. The captured dragon seemed to know what it was; it tried to wiggle and kick its way free with increasing panic. And then, two large creatures broke out into the opposite side of the clearing.

What the—? Carter thought as the creatures came into view. They were huge and muscular and covered in brown scales with fierce-looking snouts. *Were they bears? Or dragons? Or bear dragons?!* The tree released the captive into the waiting arms of a bear dragon. The other, smelling something in the air, turned toward the boys.

"Run!"

The boys took off down the path, but stopped short at the edge of another cliff, this one overlooking the ocean.

"Now where?" Carter asked.

Several dragons roamed the skies. One of them spotted the boys. It let out a cry as it circled in the sky and headed their way. The others followed. Jackson turned around; the bear dragon was charging toward them from the other direction. It was so close the ground shook. "We have to jump," he said.

Carter looked down at the water below. They were up high, even higher than the high dive at the local pool. Carter had never jumped off the high dive—he had always been too afraid.

Jackson knew what his little brother was thinking. "It'll be okay, Carter. You can do this."

Carter nodded.

"Keep your legs together and your arms tight to your chest."

Jackson gently pushed his brother off the edge and watched him fall into the water. He could feel the bear dragon approaching from behind and, up in the sky, a flying dragon was swooping down, reaching out with its claws. Jackson jumped, just narrowly escaping the dragon's grasp, and plunged into the water below.

He didn't swim to the surface right away in case the dragon was circling above waiting for him. But as he waited, he saw something coming towards him under the water—something huge!

A giant sea serpent wiggled its way toward him with tremendous speed. Jackson tried to swim away, but the serpent spit water at him—not fire like a normal dragon—but a stream of water! The force pushed Jackson back and he smacked against the cliff; water gushed up his nose.

He heard a scream, muffled in the water: "Jackson!" Out of the corner of his eye, he saw Carter, underwater, watching the scene unfold with horror.

The sea serpent continued to pin Jackson against the cliff with a stream of water as it swam toward him with an open mouth, sharp teeth, and wild, hungry eyes. The world around Jackson began to disappear until he could see nothing but the darkness of the creature's cavernous mouth.

3

Where's Campbell?

Jackson bolted up in bed. His shirt was wet with sweat and his heart was racing. *It was just a dream*, he assured himself. He breathed slowly, trying to slow his heartrate.

"No!"

He looked over and saw his little brother's eyes pop wide open. Carter was trying to 'swim' out of his bed sheets.

Jackson rushed to his bedside. "You're okay. You were having a nightmare," he explained.

Carter gave up the fight against his sheets and looked around his bedroom in relief. "Oh, *man!*" he said. "I had the craziest dream!"

"Yeah?" Jackson said. He wasn't really listening. He was still trying to recover from his own nightmare.

"I dreamed we were in this crazy world and dragons were chasing us!" Carter said.

"Funny," Jackson said absentmindedly as he headed to the bathroom. "I dreamed about dragons, too." He could still see the sea dragon's mouth closing around him.

"The dragons took Campbell away," Carter said. He was smiling as if he thought that was funny. When Jackson came out of the bathroom a few seconds later, Carter was standing over Campbell's empty mattress. "I guess she sleepwalked again."

If Campbell sleepwalked during the night, their parents knew not to wake her; that was how Jackson got slapped. It was safer to just carry her to her room and put her in bed.

Jackson shook his head as if to say, *Figures*, and then he and Carter headed downstairs.

***

The boys were eating cereal in the kitchen when their mother entered. "Where's your sister?" she asked.

"I dunno," Carter answered as if she had accused him of something.

"She's not in her room?" Jackson asked.

"Your father said she slept in your room last night."

"She did, but she wasn't there when we woke up."

"So where is she?"

Jackson just shrugged.

Their mother grimaced and shook her head as if to say, *Thanks for the help*, before heading upstairs. When she came back a little later, she was on the phone and moving much more urgently. "Is Campbell with you?" she asked into the phone. "Well, she's not in the house." She opened the sliding door that led to the back patio and walked out into the backyard. "No, she's not out here, either." She reentered the house. "I've looked everywhere. She's not here." There was a long pause. "Do you think she could have sleepwalked out of the house?"

The boys shared a look that said with Campbell, anything is possible.

"Can you take off work to help me look for her?" their mother continued. "I'll call my mother to watch the boys."

***

Carter felt a rush of nervous excitement. He was *so close* to passing Level 4 of Dragonsbane! He had been stuck on Level 3 for weeks. And now, in one day, he was about to reach Level 5. It was incredible what he could accomplish when he didn't have a little sister walking back and forth in front of him all the time or barking 'Carter' every two seconds or 'accidentally' shutting off the television on him when he was about to defeat a dragon. Dragonsbane was so much easier when you could focus and not have to stop and play Dance Party every five minutes 'to be fair to your sister.'

Carter raised his character's shield just in time to block the Green Dragon's fire, and then he slid to the left and slashed the dragon's throat with his sword. The dragon roared. It tried to blast Carter's character with fire, but with its throat cut, the fire went straight down and burned its own belly instead. Carter maneuvered for a better position and then thrust his sword into the dragon's heart and the dragon exploded into a mystical dust that rose into the air. When the dust was gone, a message came onscreen congratulating Carter for passing Level 4.

As he watched the animation that introduced Level 5, Carter rubbed his hands—they were starting to ache from playing nonstop for so long. He sighed deep and long. He was so excited just a few seconds ago. And now, with the triumph of passing a level behind him and the hard slog of passing a more difficult level in front of him, he felt kind of tired, bored even. He didn't really want to continue playing, but he also didn't want to waste this precious opportunity to play undisturbed.

The game started, but Carter's mind and heart were not in it. For as long as he could remember, he wished he could play Dragonsbane without Campbell bothering him. And now that he could, he kind of . . . sort of . . .

"I don't miss her," he blurted defensively. Still, he was so used to having her around, it was weird without her. He kept looking around as if he expected Campbell to walk by at any moment. He was distracted by the lack of distractions, and his character was easily torched by the Gold Dragon.

He sighed again, and after looking around to make sure no one was watching, he exited Dragonsbane and launched Dance Party. He chose Glo for his character and laughed because he knew, if Campbell was there, she would be furious. Glo was *her* character. But she wasn't there, so there was nothing she could do about it. *Ha!* he thought, imagining the absolute fit Campbell would throw if she knew he was playing as Glo. But then he frowned. It wasn't as funny without her there to see it. The music started and he danced his way to a new high score—with Campbell's favorite character! "She's going to be *so* mad," he said with relish. But again, it was a hollow joke without her there to get mad at him.

Carter was trying to decide what to do next, play Dance Party again or return to Dragonsbane, when he heard his parents enter the house. He turned off the game and went downstairs to find out where Campbell had been.

He was shocked to find she wasn't with his parents. His mom and dad were explaining things to his Nana. They spoke in quiet voices with sad, serious faces. Carter couldn't hear everything, but he could tell from his mother's red and weary eyes that she was very worried. He thought he heard the words 'run away.'

Carter crossed over to Jackson at the kitchen counter. "What happened?"

Jackson just shrugged.

Their mom and dad finally realized the boys were watching them. "Did you boys say anything to Campbell last night about sleeping in your room?" their father asked.

"No," Jackson answered.

"Did you kick her out?" their mother asked.

"No."

27

Their mother looked at them for a moment as if she didn't believe them. "*Carter?*"

"No! *Gees.*"

Their parents pulled Nana aside to continue their private conversation.

Carter turned to Jackson: "I told you she'd blame me."

Jackson nodded at first, but then shook his head in confusion. He remembered Carter saying that, but in his *dream.* Or was he forgetting something? "When did you say that?" he asked.

"Last night in the jungle—" Carter began before stopping himself, a little embarrassed. "Never mind. That was in my dream."

"You dreamt a dragon flew off with Campbell?"

"Yeah, I told you that."

"Did you dream about the plant biting her?"

Carter nodded.

"And the storm with all the lightning and rain and the volcanic eruptions and earthquakes?"

Carter nodded at it all.

"The dragon that took Campbell, was it white?"

"Yeah."

"And then another dragon came for us, but a tree grabbed it?"

"How do you know all this?"

"And then more dragons came after us, but we escaped by jumping off a cliff into the ocean."

"And then a giant sea serpent ate you and was about to eat me too when I woke up."

Jackson took a moment to digest it all. "I had the same dream," he said.

"That is so weird."

"No, Carter. I had the *exact* same dream. Every detail. *Exactly* the same. Weird doesn't cover it."

Carter seemed hesitant to believe it. "Did the plants bark in your dream?" he asked, trying to think of the strangest detail.

"Like wild dogs."

"Mine too." He paused to think it through. "How is that possible?"

"I don't know."

"Unless . . ." Now it was Carter's turn to get spooked. He didn't have to say it for Jackson to know what he was thinking; Jackson was thinking the same thing. What if it *wasn't* a dream. What if somehow it was all *real* and a dragon *really* did take Campbell? What if she was *really* trapped there?

4

Campbell in the Clouds

Campbell didn't want to cry, but her eyes wouldn't cooperate. They felt the situation called for tears, and eyes obey emotions more than thoughts. So tears they shed. Campbell tried with all her might to hold them back, and with nowhere else to go, they welled up in her eyes and watered down her ability to see clearly—perhaps in a desperate attempt to shield her from how dire the situation was.

But she didn't need to *see* to understand the danger. She could *feel* the dragon's claws gripping her; *feel* the cold wind blowing against her as it dragged her through the sky, *feel* the emptiness beneath her feet. Where the dragon was taking her, what it planned to do with her, she had no idea. That was the scariest part. So Campbell squeezed her eyes shut and forced the tears down her cheek where they froze to her skin in the cold air. She had to blink several times to be rid of them before she could see her surroundings clearly.

She was soaring miles high in the sky and the landscape below looked like a toy model of a valley with rivers and cliffs that all swept up into a huge mountain range. The dragon was flying toward an enormous spread of clouds that hovered in the sky beyond the mountains. They spread as wide and high as her eyes could see, like an endless wall.

A darker section of the cloud wall rumbled and crackled as they approached. Campbell heard an explosion behind her and she turned just in time to see a flaming rock headed right for her head. But then a bolt of lightning darted out from the dark clouds and struck the rock, obliterating it.

The dragon continued on, aiming for a small circle in the cloud wall where the clouds were wispy, like a fluttering curtain. The dragon flew right through it. There was a moment of blinding darkness before they exited out on the other side.

Campbell blinked several times as if she didn't trust her eyes—after all, the disobedient cowards had just been crying a moment ago. There was a whole other world in the clouds: mountain ranges, valleys, plains and plateaus, entire continents and islands all made of clouds with oceans of empty sky in between. It not only stretched out toward the horizon but upward, too, creating an endless multilayered world.

The dragon crested a small range of cloud mountains, crossed a plateau, and then swooped down into a basin completely encircled by tall cloud cliffs. A line of winged dragons stood waiting below, watching the sky eagerly. Though clearly dragons, they resembled different birds— eagles, falcons and hawks mostly, with a few here and there that looked more like owls or other birds of prey. Instead of feathers, they were covered in scales.

Her captor swept over their heads and entered the cloud cliff through another wisp of clouds. Inside was a giant cloud cavern. The only light came from sporadic lightning flashes. Down below, shadows moved like the sea in a storm. In the flickering light, she could see shapes being dragged toward a empty circle in the ground at the far end of the cavern.

Campbell's captor dropped her into the shadows, but before she landed, she was caught by a swirl of wind that wrapped itself around her like a mini-tornado and lowered her down. She tried to wrestle free, but the tornado pinned her arms to her sides and prevented her from moving. She was still a prisoner, just transferred from one captor to another.

More sky dragons swooped in, each one carrying a wingless dragon as its prisoner. Some of the captured dragons resembled horses, others had horns like elk, one looked like a rhinoceros. It was difficult to see clearly in the flickering light, but just like the sky dragons, no matter how similar they looked to other animals, they were all clearly dragons. There were wolf dragons, buffalo dragons, panther dragons—all kinds of wingless dragons, and each one was held prisoner by a swirl of wind, just like her. They did their utmost to break free and escape—kicking and tossing their heads like bucking broncos, thrusting their bodies in every direction as they fought against the tornadoes. Their angry grunts and roars competed with the howling wind for dominance of the air. The lightning continued to flicker like strobe lights; it was like being in a zoo turned violent disco.

The tornadoes proved too strong, too unbreakable, and eventually, they organized the chaos into orderly rows of subdued prisoners, and the uproar was replaced by the dull murmur of the defeated dragons struggling to catch their breath, topped by the whistling taunts of the victorious wind.

Campbell was too small and too constrained by her tornado to see anything more than the row in front of her. She heard an occasional cry of protest followed by a rush of wind, and then the line of prisoners would move forward. This was repeated over and over until the lines in front of her had thinned enough for her to foresee her fate.

Each prisoner was brought before a large dragon with a mean, vulture-looking face and brown scales with yellow tints. It surveyed the prisoner, asked it a question or two, then waved its claw and the tornado carried its prisoner through the hole in the bottom of the cloud cavern.

Where are they taking them? she wondered. And then it was her turn in front of the vulture dragon. Campbell's presence shocked the creature out of its routine. He eyeballed her with a combination of confusion and disgust.

"Who captured this creature?"

"I did, sir." Campbell's captor stepped forward.

"So while the rest of us were at war, you were out collecting pets."

The others all laughed riotously, and the dragon dropped its head in shame.

Campbell crinkled her nose. *'Pet'?!*

"Well, it's just . . ." the dragon tried to say above the laughter, "It's just . . . I mean . . . it kind of looks like a . . ." he appeared reluctant to say it. "I mean, don't you think it looks like a . . ."

They all huddled closer to Campbell, trying to figure out what she looked like.

"Oh." One of them said, and as the awareness spread, their eyes all widened as if their eyes, too, were all saying, *Oh.*

Campbell's blood rose. Her fear turned into indignation. Between the flickering lightning and their rude stares, it felt like she was being poked and prodded.

"Reginald you're not suggesting this creature is a . . ." Vulture started, but he too seemed reluctant to finish the thought.

"No, no. I'm not saying *that.* I'm just saying it looks like—kind of!—looks like one."

One what?! Campbell wondered.

"I thought Airon might want to see it," her captor added.

Vulture poured on the mockery. "Oh, by all means, Reginald, run along and tell our king you've captured a *human!*" The others laughed with him, but it was a nervous, hesitant laugh. It was the laughter of self-defense.

"I didn't say that! I never said that!" her captor protested. "Everyone knows humans are just myths!"

Campbell had had enough. "I'm not a myth. *You're* the myth!"

The dragons became silent and looked at Campbell again. She was fuming, but too small to take seriously as a threat.

"Behold the mighty human!" one of them shouted and they all burst out laughing!

"I want to go home!" Campbell shouted. She dragged the word 'home' out into a scream that was as loud and as long as her lungs could muster.

Vulture was unmoved. "Well, whatever it is, it's a beastly little thing? Throw it in the dungeon with the others. Let it scream at the wind."

He flicked his claw, and the tornado dragged Campbell away and dropped through the dark hole. After several moments of pitch blackness, they emerged out into the sky.

The dungeon was not at all what Campbell was expecting. Instead of dark and dingy cells with stone walls and iron bars, it was hundreds—if not thousands—of small clouds dotted across the sky. Above them, a blanket of storm clouds crackled and flickered menacingly—part wall, part guard towers.

The tornado whooshed over to an empty cloud and unraveled itself—disappearing outward into a gust of wind and dropping Campbell onto the cloud all in the same motion.

The prison clouds were only about fifteen square feet in size, and the larger dragons barely had enough room to stretch out. Campbell, being much smaller than a dragon, had plenty of space. But that was of little comfort. She peered over the edge of her cloud: outside of that fifteen square feet were miles of total emptiness between her and the ground below. She didn't need to be in a dark, dingy cell with stone walls and iron bars to be trapped. The emptiness was just as inescapable.

A gust of wind howled past her like a guard walking the cellblock of a prison. She hurried away from the edge of her cloud and watched the wind circle her again before it moved on to the next cloud.

That wind had a dragon's face! she realized.

The dark clouds above thundered and, together with the dragon wind, they taunted the prisoners like prison guards who bang on the cell bars with their batons as they pass. More dragon wind flew by, bullies taunting her—shouting at her, messing up her hair, pulling at her pajamas, threating to push her off the cloud at any moment.

She dropped to her knees and huddled with her stuffed panda bear. Where were Jackson and Carter? Were they captured, too, or did they escape? Would they come for her? Would they be able to find her up here in the clouds? Could they reach her—rescue her? She struggled to find hope, but instead, fear and hopelessness flowed over her like the wind. She shivered and hugged her panda bear so tightly its eyes bugged out.

"I like hugs," the panda bear said. But it looked absolutely terrified.

5

Dragonland

The boys sat at the island in the kitchen as their Nana cut up some dragon fruit for them as a late-night snack.

"After this, it's straight to bed," she said. "And I don't want any arguments." She handed them each a small plate of fruit and then shuffled away mumbling about how it was always such a fight putting them to bed and how she was in no mood for a fight tonight and how she was getting too old for this and how it was so cold in the house—why do they keep it so cold in here?—and how her gout was acting up and gees this house was a mess and why don't those boys clean up after themselves, but they are sweet boys.

"Okay," Jackson said once she was out of earshot. "Let's assume it was real and not a dream. How did it happen? What was different about last night?"

"Dad gave us the dragon statues!" Carter realized.

"Right!" Jackson said, but his excitement quickly faded. "But Campbell didn't get a dragon statue, so why would she have been there, too?" Jackson was about to eat his last piece of dragon fruit when his eyes froze on the wooden box with the Chinese writing. "But she *did* eat the dragon fruit."

Carter was just about to put another piece into his mouth when Jackson's words froze him. The piece of fruit slipped from his hands and onto his plate. "Do you think it's really *magical*?" He looked down at it as if it had suddenly become poisonous.

Jackson examined his last piece of dragon fruit and shrugged. "I guess we'll find out," he said as he tossed it into his mouth.

***

Jackson was doing his best to relax and fall asleep, but whether it was the excitement of having a fruit-paved path to a lost world of dragons, the fear of actually going back there to rescues his sister, of the absolute ruckus his brother was making in the closet, sleep was hard to come by.

"Carter, what are you *doing* in there?!"

"Trying to find my sword and shield."

"Why?"

"So I can take them with me."

"What are you talking about?"

A few more bangs and a big crash later, Carter emerged from the closet with a sword in one hand and a shield in the other.

"Campbell had her stuffed bear with her in Dragonland, remember? Maybe if we go to sleep holding something, we'll have it with us when we go back there."

Carter climbed into bed with his weapons and sorted the covers around him, trying to conceal the bulge created by the shield.

Jackson rolled his eyes. "You're more likely to poke your eye out with that thing than bring it into your dream." With that, Jackson rolled over and closed his eyes to shut out the world.

***

Their Nana shuffled back into the kitchen. "Okay, you two, it's bedtime. I don't want to hear any . . ." Her voice trailed off when she realized the boys were no longer there.

She went upstairs, assuming they were playing video games and preparing herself for a fight only to find them already asleep in bed—without any argument, without even having to tell them. She stood outside their room, not wanting to risk waking them.

Carter grunted, and she stood watching him for a moment, wondering what he was dreaming about. *Hmm*, she thought as she pondered the sight of him under the covers. *Carter's getting a little chunky. All that junk food.* And with that, she left to go watch her stories and enjoy the peace and quiet.

***

Carter was flying through a thick mist. Or was he swimming? Whatever he was doing, he was doing it in an endless sea of mist. He went faster, eager to see something, to get his bearings. An outline started to take shape—*Are those mountains?* He wondered. He raced to break through the mist when, without warning . . .

***

Carter awoke to find himself on the same black, gravelly sand in the same clearing as last time. *It's like a video game,* he thought. *I have to start over from the beginning. This must be the starting point.*

The sky was a deep, dark blue, suggesting the sun would rise soon. But for now, everything was cast in a dim light. Everything around them was asleep. The jungle was so sleepy looking it made him yawn.

"Jackson, are you awake?"

Jackson rose to his feet to find Carter standing with a shield on his arm and a sword in hand. "It worked?!" he said. Then he looked down at Carter's feet. "You went to bed with shoes on, too?!"

"The gravel hurt my feat," he explained.

Jackson looked down at his bare feet and Carter was unable to contain a smile.

Jackson knew what his brother was thinking: *You should have listened to me.* "We're wasting time," he said to change the subject. He looked for the narrow path they had taken earlier. "Come on."

"Did you have a dream before you woke up here?" Carter asked as they walked through the sleeping jungle. He spoke in a whisper, careful not to wake the dragon plants.

"Why do you ask?"

"I dreamt I was flying through the clouds. Or maybe I was swimming through a thick mist. It was hard to tell. But just when I was about to break through to the surface, I woke up here. Did you dream that, too?"

"I don't remember."

"Because I was thinking . . . what if it wasn't a dream? What if it was how we how we actually got here? Wherever here is." Carter studied the various plants and trees: the scaly tree bark, the wing-like leaves, and the snout-like heads on the plants. "Everything here looks like a dragon," he said.

Jackson nodded, but said nothing and continued on until they arrived at the cliff that overlooked the valley. It was difficult to see in the dim, early morning light, but Jackson could make out the black outline of the mountains against the deep blue sky. They looked ominous, and the memory of the dragon carrying his little sister off toward them gave him a chill.

The sky turned a lighter blue to welcome in the new day, and the black mountains turned brown. "The sun is rising," Jackson said.

Carter nodded, but as the golden light crowned the horizon, he slapped his brother on the shoulder. "Jackson," he said almost breathlessly. "That isn't a sun."

They watched as a ginormous golden dragon flew up into the sky, its three heads breathing continuous streams of fire in different directions. The wind resistance from its flight caused the fire to curve around it, almost totally encircling it, and the light from the flames shone brilliantly off its golden scales. It was so enormous and bright it lit the entire world.

"Even the *sun* is a dragon here!" Carter exclaimed.

As the dragon sun rose, more of the world came into view—the valley, the distant mountain range, and one giant mountain that rose up to meet the clouds in the sky.

"The dragon was headed for that mountain," Jackson said. He got down on his belly and peered over the edge of the cliff to see if there was a way for them to climb down. But it was a sheer drop.

As Carter waited for his brother, he had an uneasy feeling—the kind he got when he was playing a video game and sensed the game was about to surprise him with a new challenge. The hairs on his neck stood tall. He turned to find a fireball flying right at his face. He ducked behind his shield just in time, and the warmth of the fire washed over him. He peeked over his shield and spotted the culprit—a nearby dragon plant. Carter readjusted his grip on his sword, and just as the dragon plant was about to spit fire again, he chopped off its head. The plant stem swayed wildly, and fire sprayed out of it like water from a loose hose until it finally crumbled into a pile of dust. The other dragon plants eyed Carter warily, but they made no move to attack. Neither did Carter. It was an unspoken truce.

"We need to find a way down into the valley," Jackson said, rising to his feet. He led the way along the cliff's edge, occasionally stopping to peer over the side. Carter followed with his shield up, sword at the ready, and his eyes in a swivel.

They walked along the cliff to where the path turned sharply and continued along an adjacent edge. Jackson looked over the side. "Still no way to climb down," he said, as he surveyed the scene.

A river cut the valley in half and flowed into a large lake. The lake was walled in between three cliff faces: the cliff they were on, one directly opposite them, and then another, much taller one in between. The top of the middle cliff was lined with rock spires that made it look like a castle wall. About halfway down, its face was dotted with a dozen archways. Below the arches, a path ran along the cliff's face all the way to the opposite cliff where it continued past the lake and down into the valley. "Over there," Jackson said, pointing. "That's our way down."

Carter surveyed the path: it was so long, so far out of the way. It would take forever to reach the mountain that way. He looked down over the edge again. "Maybe we can jump into the lake," he suggested.

"We're too high up." Jackson said. "And we don't know how deep it is. Or what's in it," he added as he recalled the giant sea serpent that almost ate him the last time he jumped off a cliff. A haze of mist hovered over the lake's surface and steam rose into the air. "I can't even see it clearly. Is that fog or is the lake *steaming*?" He shook his head. "It's way too risky."

Jackson started off along the cliff's edge, but Carter didn't follow. "Jackson, that's the wrong direction."

"It's the only way," Jackson said with a hint of apology.

Carter still didn't follow; he turned and looked out toward the distant mountain again. He didn't say anything, but just shook his head.

Jackson returned and put his hand on his little brother's shoulder. "Don't worry, Carter. We'll find her. And we *will* rescue her."

6

Atmos

"Carter, stop!"

Campbell was aghast! Carter was playing Dance party as Glo! She watched him from a cloud that was floating above their playroom (oddly, their house had no ceiling or walls, so she could see everything). "Carter!" she shouted with horror as his score increased. Carter ignored her and played on. "Mom!" she screamed, but her voice was drowned out by a thousand dragons cheering Carter on. They were on a ring of clouds that surrounded the playroom. "He's really good," Vulture said from the cloud next to Campbell's.

Ugh, dragons are so annoying! "Mom!" she shouted again.

But her mother never came, and the score continued to go higher and higher until the words 'New High Score!' flashed onscreen. The dragons erupted into a thunderous roar of excited cheers and applause.

"No!" Campbell shouted. She jumped for the playroom, hoping to shut off the game before the high score was recorded, when . . .

***

Campbell felt a moment of weightlessness, then a jerk, a twist and a tumble. She opened her eyes to find herself in the middle of the air, staring at the ground miles below. But she wasn't falling; she was hanging upside down. A dragon tornado had caught her by her legs. Campbell was relieved—

not because she had just been rescued from falling—but because it was just a dream. Her high score was safe.

The dragon tornado dragged her back over to her cloud cell and dumped her safely on top. Then her mind turned to more immediate concerns. *I must have sleepwalked off the cloud*, she thought. *And the wind caught me.*

Campbell's mind started to race. The past day had been unbearable. Yes, this dragon prison was scary. But even worse than that, it was boring! Campbell was so bored her boredom overtook her fear. It was enough to make her angry how bored she was, but not angry enough to overcome the boredom. She couldn't wait around for her brothers to rescue her. She needed to take matters into her own hands. She needed to escape. Not only because she didn't want to be trapped here forever with an entire world of annoying dragons, but because she needed something to *do!*

She peered over the edge at the ground far below. As she did, the dragon wind jetted over and circled her cloud. But this time she didn't back away. *It didn't let me fall*, she reminded herself. If she was going to get off this cloud, that dragon wind was her best shot. She watched it with curiosity—no fear—wondering, *Can I ride it?* Back home that would have been a crazy idea, but here, where dragons existed and she could walk on clouds, why couldn't she ride the wind? She took a step closer to the edge. "I want to go home," she screamed at the dragon wind. "Do you hear me?! I want to go home!"

The dragon wind became angry—its prisoner wasn't heeding its warning. Its whistle turned into a roar as it circled her cloud faster and faster. She watched it carefully, trying to time it, then looked again at the ground miles below. *Don't worry. If you fall, it will catch you*, she assured herself. And then, when it came around again, she jumped for its 'back.' Or so she thought. The moment she jumped, the dragon wind encircled her, forming a tornado.

The dragon tornado dragged her back to her cloud, but just as it dropped her, another dragon wind charged down and grabbed her, and whisked her up towards the storm clouds. The clouds threatened her with lightning, but they didn't strike. Instead, a wispy hole opened in the dark clouds, and the dragon tornado pulled her through it, up a tunnel, and out into the sky, higher into the world of clouds.

The dragon tornado continued past the various cloud islands that spread outward and upward in the sky. They crested the edge of the uppermost cloud island, and then swept down into its wide cloud valley flanked by two cloud mountain ranges. A river flowed through the middle of the valley. *Or is that a wind stream?* Campbell wondered. *Or both?*

The distance between the mountain ranges narrowed and the valley thinned into a tight passageway. Two dark clouds hovered above the entrance to the pass like guards in a watchtower. Behind them rose a giant cloud mountain that sat atop the cloud world like a capstone on a pyramid. As Campbell approached, the cloud guards flickered with the threat of lightning. The dragon tornado passed beneath them, through the opening, and out into a broad expanse of empty sky that surrounded the giant mountain.

Like a moat, Campbell thought.

They crossed the sky moat and entered a large tunnel in the cloud mountain's base. The tunnel led into a gigantic cloud cave lit with flickering lightning. The dragon tornado dragged Campbell up through a tunnel in the top of the cave.

After a long dark climb, they emerged into the center of an enormous dragon pit that sat atop the cloud mountain. It was as if someone had plugged the top of volcano with a football stadium. Dragons—thousands of them—were seated on tiers of floating clouds that rose upward and outward like stadium seating. Several rainbows crossed above, forming a cathedral ceiling. At the far end of the stadium, two narrow clouds dumped thick blankets of rain, concealing whatever lay behind them. The rain seeped into the cloud floor, where it formed an undercloud river than ran half the length of the stadium and collected into a undercloud pool in the center. The pool reflected the light that passed through the rainbow, so that the ground floor was covered in a multicolored haze.

The dragon tornado paraded Campbell around the ring so the crowd could get a good look at her. She returned their curious stares. There were all kind of various-looking dragons, each one with different colored scales. There were swan-looking dragons with scales that looked like shining pearls, raven-looking dragons with scales like onyx crystals. Some dragons had scales with blueish tints that made it look like they were covered in aquamarine gemstones, others shone with hints of ruby, others with touches of emerald. There were even multi-colored dragons that looked like parrots.

As she passed, they whispered to each other out of the sides of their dragon mouths, not taking their beady dragon eyes off her for a second. Then a lone voice cried out, "Behold the mighty human!" and the crowd erupted in laughter.

Campbell recognized the voice from before. *Get a new joke*, she thought.

After it circled the stadium, the dragon tornado dragged Campbell the length of the hall toward the other end; the two rain clouds drifted away from each other and their dense rainfall split apart like a drawn curtain. Behind the veil of rain was a large alcove, its cloud walls dotted with tiny ice nuggets that sparkled like diamonds.

On a raised ledge, perched on a giant cloud throne that also sparkled with numerous gem-like ice nuggets, sat a sky dragon twice the size of all the others. And unlike the others, there was nothing resembling a bird in him; he was all dragon. His scales shined with a purple tint and his eyes looked like purple gemstones. A circle of triangular purplish scales grew out of his head to form what looked like a scaly crown. Although no one introduced him, she guessed this was their leader, the one they called Airon.

He flicked his claw and the dragon tornado unraveled itself and flew away, giving his majesty a better look at the small creature before him. In an instant, Airon's expression changed from curious to alarmed, though it was hard to be sure—he did have a dragon face after all.

"Was it alone?" he asked, turning to her captor who stood off to the side next to Vulture.

"There were two others, Sire. Like this one, only a little bigger with shorter manes."

"Only three," Airon said to himself more than to the others. "And where are the other two?"

"They jumped into the ocean," Vulture said. "We presumed the Mers captured them, but according to our envoy, the creatures escaped them as well."

"So they are still on the loose." Airon paused for a moment to consider what this meant.

Campbell was relieved to hear her brothers had escaped, but then she frowned: it was unfair that only *she* got caught. At least *Carter* should have been captured, too. To be fair.

Airon had been watching her and seemed intrigued by the range of emotions that crossed her face. "Where's Felton?" he called to the entire stadium. "Felton!"

There was a shuffle at the far end as a small dragon up in the cheap seats tried to make his way through the crowd. "Coming, Sire."

The crowd's rowdy jeers turned into confused whispers. They were expecting this gathering to be all fun and games, but their king seemed to be taking it seriously.

Airon raised a claw and from out of the darkness behind him came a leather-bound book flying through the air. It looked small compared to him, the way a stamp would look to a human. It stopped and floated in mid-air before him. He flicked his claw again, and the pages flipped over until he found what he was looking for. With another flick of the claw, the book floated over to Campbell and hovered a few feet in front of her. It looked like someone's diary and was opened to a hand drawing of dragon fruit.

"Did you eat of the sacred fruit?" Airon asked.

Campbell knew he was asking about dragon fruit, but she did her best not to show it. Instead, she did what she always did when she suspected she might be in trouble: she shrugged. "I dunno." Airon's eyes narrowed and Campbell could feel them on her like a harsh spotlight. But she held her ground.

By this point the small, dovish-looking dragon from the cheap seats arrived. While he was much smaller than the other dragons, he was still twice Campbell's size. He had dull white scales, but under his chin was a gray-colored patch of scales that looked like a beard; it made him look older and wiser, less beastly than the others. *Give him a pair of glasses and he'd look like a fussy old librarian*, Campbell thought.

With a flick of his claw, Airon closed the book and passed it to the small dragon. "Felton, our knowledge of humans is centuries old. Question this creature and find out how their capabilities have grown and evolved. How much of a threat do they pose? It appears humans have found their way back to Dragonland. I want to know why."

Upon hearing Airon's words, confused and horrified gasps flew around the stadium like angry wasps.

"Yes!" Airon bellowed to the assembled crowd. "Humans are real. Their realm, Earth, is real. And the myths you have heard really *did* happen. Do not let this creature's puny stature deceive you . . ."

Puny?! Campbell thought. *Man, dragons are rude!*

". . . The return of humans to Dragonland poses a serious threat!"

Airon sighed, and his voice became more somber as he told his tale: "For eons, we dragons travelled beyond the mist to raid and plunder their world. Only Dragons could cross the mist. So after every raid, we retreated safely back to Dragonland.

"Then, a human named Beowulf slayed a dragon and its blood soaked into the Earth. From that spot grew a tree bearing a sacred fruit. Eating of this fruit gave humans the power of the dragon. When they slept, and their human minds were at rest, the dragon power took over and guided them through the mist to Dragonland.

"Only a few humans came at first. But over time, they came in greater numbers and with more advanced weaponry. We fought terrible battles with them, *here!* In our own lands! We captured one of these humans and learned they had begun growing thousands of these dragon fruit trees all over Earth. Some humans just wanted to visit Dragonland to learn the ways of the dragon, but others planned to invade with entire armies and destroy us.

"So, we attacked them first, and burned all of Earth's dragon fruit orchards to the ground. To further confuse the humans, we flew across Earth dropping seeds for false dragon fruit trees, ones not grown in dragon's blood, so the humans would believe the sacred fruit had lost its power.

"Of course, I could not risk another dragon getting slayed, lest its blood give life to a new tree and the cycle begin anew. So I clouded the mist so dragons could no longer pass through it to Earth. And then I allowed the passage of time to turn these events into myths, and the truth was lost in the past.

Wait! The stories about dragons are actually real?! Campbell wondered in amazement. She looked at Airon and imagined him flying through her hometown and raiding her school.

"Now it appears the humans have returned," Airon continued. "For what purpose, we do not yet know. But I do know this . . ." He looked down at Campbell with mean, hard eyes. "Last time, *all* of our troubles started with just *one* of them. We cannot allow these humans to escape and tell their tales or more humans will follow until all of Dragonland is under siege once again. Find the others and bring them to me, bound by the wind and trembling with fear!"

There was a storm of fluttering wings and war cries, and Campbell turned to see every dragon in the stadium take to the sky.

7

The Attack

The boys reached the point where their cliff joined the larger center cliff and the path forked in two different directions. "That way probably leads back to the clearing," Jackson said, pointing down the path that cut through the jungle. He shook his head with frustration as he realized they walked all the way around the edge when they could have just cut through the middle.

Carter looked out toward the mountain range in the distance and sighed; it was even further away than before. Then he bucked himself up and continued on with renewed energy.

They crossed a small land bridge to where the path ran along the face of the center cliff. On their right, the cliff wall towered high above them, blocking out the sky. To their left was a sharp drop into the boiling lake below.

When they passed the first archway in the cliff face, they slowed down to look inside. The archway was actually a tunnel that cut through the cliff wall, but they couldn't see what was on the other end—just bright light. They continued on.

As they walked, the sound of crashing waves threatened them from below. It was difficult to see with all the steam, but it looked as if waves in the lake were beating against the cliff face.

"Do you hear that?"

"It's just the waves," Jackson said.

The Attack

Carter had stopped and was looking out towards the distant mountains. He shook his head. "No. *That*."

In the blink of an eye, darkness swallowed the horizon. The mountains disappeared, only flickering back into view with the occasional lightning strike. The wind picked up and became furious, almost as if it was boiling. Dark clouds gathered and rumbled like huge catapults being dragged to the battle line. Something cried out and then hundreds— thousands!—of dragons charged forward with the storm clouds in tow, dragging fury and darkness across the sky. They were headed right for the boys.

"Hurry," Jackson shouted. The boys raced along the path. They had almost reached the next arch when a lightning bolt struck the ground in front of them and cut a gash in the path; rock tumbled down over the edge. The boys looked up to see a dark cloud flashing hot as if it was recharging for another lightning strike. Rain began to pound down on them.

Carter didn't hesitate—he ran as fast as he could and jumped over the gash. Jackson followed. They rushed into the arch a second before a lightning bolt blew away the path in front of it, trapping them inside.

The boys were breathing so heavily they couldn't talk. Seconds passed before Carter managed to say through struggled breath, "Those are the same dragons as before." He walked back toward the opening with his sword and shield raised.

"Carter, are you nuts? Those things are a *lot* bigger than the dragon plants. You can't fight them."

"Maybe we should let them capture us? They'll take us right to Campbell."

"If they capture us, we'll be trapped here just like her. Come on." Jackson led the way up the tunnel. With all the storm clouds, there was no light at the end, just a lighter darkness.

They heard thunder, crashing rocks and the cries of battle, but they couldn't see any of it except for the occasional flash of lightning. All the action was happening at the other end of the tunnel, on the opposite side of the cliff wall. Jackson and Carter crept up the tunnel, staying close to the sides and out of sight. Water began to trickle down the tunnel floor.

They heard what sounded like cannon fire, followed by a howl, and then something crashed to the ground at the edge of the tunnel—right in front of them!

Lightning was flashing like a strobe light, giving them intermittent glimpses of the fallen creature: a winged dragon. It struggled to its feet with a pained groan and was about to jump into the air when two other creatures pounced on it. At first, Carter thought they were tigers, but then he realized they were actually dragons. They were striped orange and black like tigers, and they didn't have wings, but everything else about them was all dragon. *Everything here is a dragon*, he reminded himself.

As they watched the scene unfold, the boys crept back to stay out of sight. More water began to run down the tunnel floor.

The tiger dragons pinned their captive to the ground until a bear dragon approached. It grabbed the winged dragon in its arms and pinned it to its chest. It was about to turn and carry its prisoner away, when it turned back, stared down the tunnel, and gave a low growl.

Jackson and Carter took another quiet step back. More water began to flow down the tunnel. The bear dragon looked up at the sky, then at the water flowing into the tunnel, then toward the boys. It gave a last low growl before carrying its prisoner away.

More water flowed into the tunnel. The lightning continued to flash like a strobe light. In a flash, they saw the two tiger dragons follow the bear dragon, then a sweep of darkness, and then another flash: the tiger dragons were back, standing at the edge of the tunnel.

"Can they see us?"

"Shh."

The tiger dragons answered with a growl, but they didn't come any closer. More water flowed into the tunnel. The tiger dragons roared again. Then, in a flash, they were gone. The boys waited for several flashes—light, dark, light—to make sure the tiger dragons were really gone for good.

"Phew, that was close," Carter said.

"Why didn't they come after us?" Jackson wondered.

More water flowed into the tunnel. It was up to the boys' knees now, making it difficult for them to keep their balance.

"Uh-oh," Jackson said, looking down at the flowing water.

"What?"

"This isn't a tunnel. It's a gutter!"

The flow of the water became faster and stronger. Jackson struggled to keep his footing. He dropped to all fours and looked around the tunnel for somewhere to escape to or something to grab onto. They tried with all their might to hold on, but it was no use. The water carried them away down the tunnel. They flew out of the arch and soared into the air before splashing down into the lake below.

The water was hot, but not scalding—probably because of all the cold rain falling into it. But there was so much steam they could barely see ten feet away.

Carter had landed near a rock. He swam over to it and climbed on top. He scanned the water for his brother but couldn't see him through the steam. "Jackson?!"

"Carter?! Where are you?!"

"On a rock! Can you see me?!" He waved his hands through the air.

"Keep shouting! I'll swim for your voice!"

Carter heard splashing before he saw Jackson swimming toward him, barely visible through the haze.

As Carter watched his brother swim, urging him on, he heard a loud whooshing sound. He looked beyond Jackson to see a giant wave headed for his brother. As it came nearer, Carter realized the wave looked like the head of a dragon with a snout in front and spikes jetting out from the back. It might have been water—but it was shaped like a dragon. *Everything here is a dragon.* "Jackson, look out!" But it was too late. The dragon wave opened its mouth and swallowed Jackson whole. "Jackson!"

Another wave passed by and reached out for Carter with what looked like a giant water claw. Carter ducked, just narrowly escaping its clutches.

He popped back up to see another, much larger wave headed right for him; it was large enough to swallow both him and the rock whole. It reminded Carter of being at the beach, bodyboarding in the ocean when a large wave—one much larger than all the others—appears out of nowhere. The only escape was to dive under it. Carter stepped to the edge of the rock and waited for the dragon wave to approach. *Now!* he told himself as it was almost upon him. He dove off the rock, but instead of feeling the bite of cold water, he felt a stabbing pain in his shoulders, followed by a violent jerk upward. As he rose above the mist, he realized one of the flying dragons had him in its claws.

Carter's emotions raced from hope to fear to resolve. *He'll take me to Campbell,* he realized. *I can't help Jackson right now*, he thought as he scanned the water below, looking for his brother. *But maybe I can help her.*

The dragon rose above the mist toward the cliff—so much water was pouring out of its arches, it reminded Carter of a dam. A lightning flash set off what looked like an explosion of light from beyond the cliff wall, but it vanished quickly into darkness. Then, as they soared higher into the sky, another lightning strike came and Carter saw sharp beams jutting up into the sky in various directions like an explosion that had been frozen into crystals of solid light. *What is that?* he wondered before the dragon swooped off in the opposite direction and headed for the giant mountain in the distance.

Don't worry, Campbell, he thought. *I'm coming.*

There was a blast that sounded like cannon fire and Carter felt something hot whiz by behind him. He looked down to see a volcano was shooting lava rock at the flying dragon and another rock was headed right for him. Carter grabbed onto the claws and pulled himself up just in time to dodge a lava rock as it went shooting by. The rock hit the dragon right in the gut. The dragon squealed in pain and its claws loosened their grip. Carter felt a moment of weightlessness followed by a strong pull downward.

His heart leapt in his chest—he was falling! He caught short glimpses of sky and ground as he tumbled through the air, and with each turn the ground was getting closer. Adrenaline pulsed through his veins and his heart pounded in his chest like a frightened bird in a cage. And just as he was about to smack into the ground . . .

***

"No!"

Carter threw out his arms to brace himself for the impact, but instead of protecting himself from the ground, he just pushed his pillow off the bed and onto the floor.

"Carter, what's wrong?" he heard, and then he felt a bright light. He opened his eyes to find his father standing over him.

"Dad, they got Jackson!" he shouted.

"It's okay, Carter, it was just a nightmare."

Carter looked over at Jackson's empty bed, the fear still pulsing through him. "Then where is he?!"

Only then did his father realize Jackson's bed was empty. "Carter, what is going on? Where did Jackson go?" Carter was too trapped in his own thoughts to hear his father, much less answer him. "Where is your brother?!"

Carter knew it would sound unbelievable, but he didn't know what else to say, what else to call a place where everything was a dragon. It took all of Carter's strength to get the word out of this mouth: "Dragonland."

8

Merantis

I can still breathe, Jackson realized with relief. That struck him as the weirdest part—not that a dragon-looking wave had just swallowed him whole, carried him downriver and dragged him out to sea—but that he could breathe underwater. The dragon wave, which looked more like a current now that they were underwater, was dragging him further away from shore and deeper into the sea. But once he realized he wasn't going to drown, Jackson relaxed—at least a little. He *was* still a prisoner.

He was in the middle of a long line of the same bizarre creatures he and Carter has seen from the tunnel—dragons without wings that resembled different types of animals. Each one was held captive by a dragon current.

When they reached the edge of the continental shelf, they dove down further and crossed a broad underwater plain. Off in the distance Jackson saw what looked like a giant coral reef stretching as wide and as high as he could see. Rays of light streamed down from above which made some areas visible, but others murky. As they neared the reef, the water grew even darker. Jackson looked up and saw that they were passing underneath a blanket of seaweed. Only, much like the plants in the forest, the seaweed was alive with wing-like leaves and snout-like mouths. One of the animal dragons broke free from its current, and the nearby seaweed swam down and wrapped itself around the creature until all Jackson could see was a squirming pod of seaweed.

The dragon current dragged Jackson towards a large opening in the coral wall. As he got closer, Jackson noticed the rim of the opening was dotted with holes. From these emerged the heads of large dragon eels; they spat currents of water like guardrails to help keep the prisoners in line. As Jackson passed through the opening, smaller dragon eels darted out from their holes and snapped at him.

Beyond the reef wall were hundreds of coral structures, some flat and broad, others narrow and tall, they covered the sea plain like an underwater city. It was difficult to see them in any detail; very little sunlight reached these depths. It was a city of jagged shades and shadows.

The dragon-current carried Jackson into the largest of the coral structures. Glowing jellyfish-like creatures dripped from the ceiling like chandeliers, lighting the interior. Amassed inside were creatures Jackson could only describe as merdragons—half fish, half dragon. Some had fishlike tails and wing-like fins with gills like a shark. Others looked more like squid dragons and there were smaller vicious looking creatures that Jackson would have described as barracuda dragons.

The largest creature of all rested on a giant bed of seaweed at the far end of the cave. It was all dragon, but the sea serpent kind: huge, long and scaly, with a ridge along its spine that ran all the way up to her thick head where it curled into crown of scales.

The sea dragon lowered her head and slithered closer, so close all Jackson could see were her two giant eyes. She took a long look at him, then spoke with so much force it was like Jackson had been sprayed with a firehose. At least Jackson assumed she had spoken. Her language sounded similar to how dolphins and whales sing, only this was nowhere near as melodious.

Upon her order, the dragon current dragged Jackson out of the structure and through a maze of coral walls. Jackson looked up and saw the layer of seaweed floating overhead had grown even thicker here. Almost no light made it through, and where it did, it cut through the water like laser beams. Here and there, Jackson could see what looked like prison cells formed in the coral with various creatures trapped inside. When the dragon current released him into an empty cell, Jackson swam as fast as he could for the surface, but before he got far, the coral grabbed him and held him down until it eventually enclosed around him. He could barely move, nor see much of anything in the dim light. But he could hear. And the sea around him was haunted with the ghost-like screams of the other prisoners.

It's okay, Jackson told himself. *Eventually you'll wake up back home, safe in your bed.* But as time went on, he thought of Campbell. She never woke up. Panic squeezed his heart as he started to understand his situation. The screams of the other imprisoned dragons swirled around him like howling sea ghosts. This wasn't a dream; it was *real*. And just like Campbell, he might be trapped here. Forever.

9

The Interrogation

Campbell was starting to miss her cloud prison. Sure, Felton's study was a lot nicer than the sky dungeon; it felt more homey—more human. But it also had Felton. And he was *so* boring! Even more boring than *prison*. He just kept asking her *boring* questions. And he was so *annoying*, too, which made the boredom so much worse.

He started by asking her why she was with the Terras. "Are the humans seeking an alliance with them?"

"I only know one Tara and I am *not* with her," Campbell said. "She told *everyone* I liked Braden because I gave him my sandwich, but I only gave it to him because it had mustard on it. Mustard is gross."

"Braden?"

"I don't *like* him."

"I didn't say you did."

"Then why do you keep asking me about him. Oh my gosh, that's all you ever want to talk about is Braden, Braden, Braden. I think *you* like him!"

"I only asked one question—"

"Braden and Felton, sitting in a tree . . ."

Felton slammed his tail hard against the ground, and steam rose from his snout. "Enough. I am just trying to understand why giving Braden mustard led you to declare war on the Terras."

"There's only one Tara. And I'm not at *war* with her. I just don't want to be her friend anymore."

"Because of the mustard?"

Campbell groaned as if she was tired of having to explain it. "Because everyone thinks I like Braden now—even *you*—and it's all her fault!"

"So . . . this Terra is another human?"

"Oh my gosh. *Yes!*"

"And they *call* her Terra?"

"Yes!"

"Interesting."

"She is so *not* interesting. She's annoying!"

"I wonder if she's connected to our Terras in some way."

"Who are your Taras?"

"They are our mortal enemies. We've been at war with them for centuries. They are barbarians—you saw what they did the day we captured you!"

"I saw a storm."

"What do you mean a *storm*?"

"Lightning, wind, waves. You know, a *storm*. And a volcano erupted!"

"That wasn't a storm. That was a battle. The volcano is how they attack us; they shoot their lava rocks into the sky to scatter our clouds and strike our air guard."

"Why?"

"The Terras have been at war with the Mers for eons. We had remained neutral, but then the Terras began invading our territory, building mountains that rose all the way up to Atmos. We had no choice but to join forces with the Mers and start defending ourselves. We've been at war with them ever since."

"Their mountains reach up to the clouds?" she asked excitedly. *If they can use the mountains to get up here, maybe I can use them to get down*, she thought to herself.

Felton paused; he could see her mind was swirling. *She certainly is asking a lot of questions,* he thought. *Like a spy.* "Enough!" he said firmly. "I'm the one asking the questions here."

"Your questions are boring!"

"Would you rather go back to the sky dungeon?" he threatened.

"I don't care. At least then I wouldn't have to answer all your *boring* questions."

Felton faltered and Campbell sensed an opening. She softened her tone. "Oh, Felton, you're doing it all wrong. This isn't how you have a conversation with a human!"

"It isn't?"

"No, silly." Campbell's voice was as sweet as cherry pie. "If you want to learn about humans, Felton, you should invite me to take tea with you."

"What do you mean 'take tea'? What is tea? And where do we take it?"

"Oh, Felton. You have so much to learn about humans."

"That's why I'm asking you these questions!"

"Then, we must have a tea party."

***

Felton and Campbell sat at a small cloud table. There was no tablecloth which disappointed Campbell to no end, but there was nothing to be done about it. At least there were cups. They were not proper teacups, which was also a disappointment, but they would have to do.

Felton watched as Campbell placed her stuffed panda bear on the chair next to him, and then set the table for the three of them before sitting down herself.

"See? Isn't this nice?"

"What is this called again?"

"It's a tea party. This is what humans do when they need to have an important conversation. They talk over tea."

Campbell poured what she insisted was tea but what Felton highly suspected was nothing more than air. She took a sip, but noticed Felton was just staring stupidly into his cup. "Try it, Felton," she said, encouragingly.

"What is it?" he asked, examining the empty cup.

"It's tea."

"It looks very similar to air."

"Oh, Felton. It's not real tea. It's pretend tea. You have to pretend."

"But why? Why don't we drink real tea? Whatever that is."

"Because that's not how you play the game. Here, have some more," she poured more air into his teacup, despite the fact that Felton had yet to drink any.

"So this is a game? How do you win?"

"You win because it's fun?"

"It doesn't seem very fun?"

Campbell pouted. "You sound like Carter." She waited to make sure Felton understood being like Carter was bad. "Now. What do you want to talk about?"

Despite the tea, the conversation only got worse. Felton thought he was so smart, but everything he believed about humans was all wrong. For example, he thought humans had kings and queens. Campbell had to explain to him that they had presidents, and a president could be a man or a woman. He thought they all rode around on horses and in chariots and she had to explain that they rode around in cars and buses and trains and airplanes. Mentioning airplanes was a huge mistake. It led to a really, *really* long argument about whether humans could fly. Then he started asking her all about human weapons. She didn't know as much as he wanted to learn and for that he accused her of "withholding information." But everything she did know he didn't believe anyway. At one point, she asked him what kind of weapons *he* had, and he refused to tell her. He just accused her of trying to "gather intelligence." She wasn't sure what he meant, but it sounded like he was calling her stupid. "Don't be rude!" she snapped.

If anything, Felton was the one who needed to gather more intelligence. Every time she mentioned something, she had to take *forever* explaining it to him. Speaking with him was so *exhausting*. He didn't know anything about *anything*. He didn't know about dancing or video games or TVs or iPads—

"What's an iPad?"

"You watch videos on it."

"What's a video?"

"Like a movie."

"What's a movie?"

"It's a story you can watch." Felton was still trying to make sense of this, but Campbell didn't want to wait for him to ask another one of his annoying questions, so she continued: "You can also play games on it."

"On a movie?"

"*No.* On an *iPad*. You can read books on it too."

"So it's a table?"

"No, it's a *tablet*. It can hold thousands and thousands of books."

"That tablet must be the size of a mountain."

"It isn't. It's the size of a single book."

Felton gave her a long, suspicious look. "You disappoint me with your lies, human."

"I'm not lying!"

"Enough! I will hear no more fanciful tales about your magical tablets, auto-chariots and humans flying through the sky on '*air* plains'!"

"If you're not going to believe anything I say, then I don't even know why I should talk to you. Talk to him, instead." And with that she grabbed her stuffed panda off the chair and thrust it into Felton's face.

"You dare insult me by suggesting I talk to your *toy*!"

Campbell squeezed the panda bear's stomach. "I like hugs!" it said.

Felton was dumbfounded. He looked like he was about to ask the stuffed bear a question when he paused, afraid of looking foolish.

Campbell seized the opportunity to take control: "Felton, what are we doing here? I thought you were supposed to be learning about humans. But apparently, you already know *everything* there is to know about humans. You don't need *me* to teach you anything. So you might as well just let me go, and you can go back and tell your king you didn't need to talk to me because you already know everything." She rose and started for the exit. "Come on. Take me home. Come on. You don't need me. You already know everything."

"I cannot do that!"

"Do you want *me* to tell Airon? I'd be happy to tell him how you think you already know everything."

"No."

"Why not? Because Airon will get *mad* at you? He's going to be mad at you anyway because you're not listening to me. You're not learning anything."

"I cannot let you go," Felton repeated, not knowing what else to say.

"Well, then it seems to me that if you don't want to get in trouble with Airon, you better start listening to me. So what's it going to be?"

From the look on Felton's face, Campbell knew he agreed, even if he was too proud to admit it. He exhaled, long and slow before saying, "Fine. Tell me more about—"

"No. You had your turn and it got us nowhere. I'm the expert on humans, so I decide what you learn." She let her words hang in the air to make sure Felton knew who was boss.

"Okay," he said, defeated.

***

Felton watched Campbell and tried to imitate her movements, he raised his arms and waved them in the air, then turned around in a circle. He didn't know what he was doing or *why* this was supposed to be fun. But, and he would never admit this to another living dragon, he was kind of enjoying it. More importantly, the creature was talking again—even more freely than before.

"Am I doing it correctly?"

Felton was a terrible dancer, but Campbell wanted to be encouraging. "You're getting much better."

"What is this called again?"

"Dance Party."

"And all humans do this?"

"All the best ones do. Only people like Carter don't like Dance Party."

"You speak of this Carter as if he's worse than mustard."

"Oh my gosh, so much worse than mustard. He's so annoying. All he wants to do is play Dragonsbane all day."

"Dragonsbane?!" Felton exclaimed. But Campbell failed to note the alarm in his voice. "Tell me more."

"Oh my gosh, I can't even deal." And with that Campbell went on and on and on about all the horrible things Carter had ever done to her, properly exaggerated for dramatic effect, of course.

10

Courage, Carter

Carter slowly descended the stairs. Most of the lights in the house were off, making it easy to stay in the shadows. He heard the television playing in the living room, and assumed his parents were watching a movie. That was going to make it more difficult to get the dragon fruit unseen. Sneaking into the kitchen wasn't the problem. The light in the refrigerator was the problem. The moment he opened the door it would shine like a silent alarm announcing his crime.

*

Carter's parents had assumed Jackson went looking for Campbell, and Carter was lying to cover for him. They demanded Carter tell them where his brother was. And the more he said "Dragonland," the more frustrated they become until finally they just sent him to his room.

"Can I have some dragon fruit to take with me," he had asked.

"No. Not until you tell us where you brother is."

Carter didn't bother saying Dragonland again. It was no use. Instead he trekked upstairs to his room, his head down, his belly in a knot of tangled emotions.

He had to admit he was a little relieved when they told him he couldn't have the dragon fruit. It meant he wouldn't have to go back to Dragonland all by himself. He laid in bed for an hour, staring at the ceiling, unable to sleep, telling himself it wasn't his fault, that he wasn't abandoning his brother and sister. But despite it all, he knew he couldn't leave them there without at least *trying* to save them. He had to go back which meant he had to eat dragon fruit. It didn't matter if he got caught, as long as he was able to make it to the fridge and eat a few pieces first.

*

Carter's mind was so preoccupied on the refrigerator light that he almost didn't realize the front door was opening right in front of him. He dove into the dining room and crawled around the corner just as his father entered, leaving the door open.

Carter's mother was speaking with someone on the front stoop, but he couldn't make out the words. He crawled over to the window and peeked outside. There were two police officers standing in the courtyard—a man and a woman. The woman was writing as his mother spoke.

"Here you go, officer," his father said as he returned and handed a small photo to the policeman.

"Okay," the policewoman said as her partner took a look at the photo. "And what's the best number to reach you?"

His parents were outside! This was his opportunity! He raced to the kitchen and was about to open the refrigerator when he heard the front door close and his parents walking his way. He crawled on his belly and hid behind the island in the center of the kitchen. If they came in to get something to eat, he was a goner. But luckily, they passed right by and went into the adjacent living room.

He peeked around the island to see what they were doing. They both looked way too distracted to notice him. So, he cracked open the refrigerator door and, without even looking, reached inside and grabbed the container of cut-up dragon fruit. He popped the lid, shoved a few pieces in his mouth, and slipped the container back into the fridge. He didn't wait around to see if he had been found out, but instead crawled as fast as he could out of the kitchen, chewing along the way. He slipped upstairs to his room where he finally swallowed the dragon fruit.

Unbeknownst to Carter, he was nowhere near as sneaky as he thought he was. His mother never saw him, but she did see the light from the open fridge just before Carter closed the door. Luckily for him, she was in no rush to scold him. So he was able to put on his shoes, and tuck himself into bed with his best available weapon—a nerf gun—in hand, before she entered his room and turned on the light.

"*Mom*," he whined. "I was asleep."

"Yeah, right." She took a moment to survey the scene and noticed the disfigured shape under his bed covers. She pulled back his sheets revealing his nerf gun. Without a word, she took it from him.

"I need that!"

"Carter, stop it."

"I ate the dragon fruit. When I fall asleep, I'll wake up back in Dragonland. I need a weapon!"

"Carter! That's enough!"

"Why don't you believe me?"

"Why don't you tell the truth?"

"You *never* believe me. I need you to *believe* me—Jackson and Campbell need you to believe me." He was on the verge of tears.

His mother sighed, then softened and looked at him with sad eyes that wondered why he was so committed to this story. She had always stressed to him that, when she punished him, she was doing it to teach him to do the right thing, to be a good person. He would appreciate that in time, when he was older and reaped the benefit of those lessons. But maybe right now he didn't need to be taught a lesson; maybe he just needed to be heard and feel supported.

"Okay," she said, wiping a tear from his face. "Tell me about Dragonland."

Carter, with renewed hope, sat up in bed to tell his tale. "After we ate the dragon fruit the night dad came home, we woke up in Dragonland and a dragon took Campbell. Jackson and I thought it was just a dream at first, but Campbell was really gone. And then, after Jackson and I ate more dragon fruit, we ended up back there. Everything there is a dragon—the plants are dragons, the trees are dragons, there are even water dragons! We were on our way to rescue Campbell when a dragon wave captured Jackson. And when I woke up, *Jackson* was gone. They're trapped there! So I ate more dragon fruit so I could go back to rescue them, but I'm going to be all by myself! I need a weapon!" And with that, Carter burst into tears.

His mother was still way too much of an adult to believe such a story, but it was clear to her that Carter's emotions were real. *This must be his way of dealing with his brother and sister's disappearance*, she told herself. In her own grief, she had lost sight of how difficult this must be for him, and she was touched that he was so concerned for his brother and sister.

"And you're going to try to fight these dragons with a nerf gun?" she asked.

"It's all I have," he said through his tears.

She looked at the clock on his nightstand; the stores were still open. "Come on, put your clothes on," she said.

"Why?"

"Because if you're going to fight dragons, you're going to need a better weapon than this."

***

They started in the camping section. His mother picked out a backpack that already came with the essentials like a flashlight and canteen. Then they went to the sports section where she began looking through the skateboard equipment.

Carter was looking at the pellet rifles when his mother joined him. "I got you elbow and knee pads and a helmet," she said. "Not exactly knight's armor, but they'll provide some protection."

"Can I get this?" Carter asked, handing her a pellet rifle.

"Aren't dragon scales supposed to be as tough as armor?" she asked.

He nodded.

"Well, I doubt a pellet gun will do you much good." She put the pellet rifle back and looked around some more. "What about a paintball gun?"

"That's not going to hurt a dragon."

"True. But nothing we can buy here is going to actually *slay* a dragon, right? But shoot enough paintballs at its face and you might be able to blind it, at least long enough to escape."

Carter smiled and nodded. It was a good idea. He picked out the largest one they had.

"That looks kind of heavy," she said. "Didn't you say you had a long walk? I'd get something lighter to carry."

He nodded: another good point. He picked out another paintball gun that was lighter but carried the same amount of ammo. He grabbed more refill canisters and dropped them in the cart. "Can we get one for Jackson, too?" he asked.

This is starting to get expensive, his mother thought. But she didn't argue. She figured she could always return it all later. "Sure," she said.

When she decided to help Carter prepare for his journey to Dragonland, she hoped it would help set him at ease. She was surprised at how much it was helping *her*—helping to distract her from her fear and helplessness. But Carter didn't seem comforted at all. He had thanked her for helping him, and that made her feel good, but the more they shopped, the more nervous he became.

I hope I'm doing the right thing, she told herself.

***

"Carter, what are you doing?" his father said, seeing his son in bed with a helmet on. He pulled back the bed sheets to reveal Carter was also wearing shoes, kneepads, elbow pads, and was hugging a backpack and two paintball guns to his chest.

"I told him he could," his mother explained.

His father looked at his mother in disbelief, but she nodded as if to say, *Trust me.* He shrugged. "Okay," he said as he tucked Carter back in and kissed him on the forehead.

"I'll explain later," his mother whispered after his father had joined her by the bedroom door.

I hope I didn't make things worse, she thought while contemplating Carter's pained face. This wasn't a game for him, she realized; he seemed to *really* believe it. A horrifying thought came to her unbidden: what if he's not lying? What if he's—? She didn't want to finish the thought. Whatever his ailment, it was caused by stress and grief, and right now, the best thing she could do for him would be to help settle his nerves and get him through the night.

She looked down at their dog Bailey who stood between her and her husband. She imagined Bailey was thinking the same thing: *Why does Carter look so worried?*

"Go on, Bailey," she said quietly, and the golden retriever jumped onto Carter's bed and snuggled up with him.

Carter, more asleep than awake, reflexively put an arm around Bailey. His other arm hugged his backpack and paint guns as if the fate of the world rested on them.

His mother stroked his forehead and kissed him again. Then she grabbed her husband by the hand, turned off the light, and they left the room.

Despite his fear, despite his nerves, despite being aware there was a really good chance he might never come back, might never see his room again, might never see his home again, might never see his parents again or his friends, that he might be trapped in Dragonland forever just like his brother and sister, despite all that, Carter fell asleep.

11

The Spy

It took some time for Jackson's panic to settle down and for his eyes to adjust to the darkness. Finally, he could see more of his surroundings, including the creature being held in the cell opposite him. It was staring right at him.

The creature moved its mouth and a bubble floated out towards Jackson. The bubble popped on his face and when it did, Jackson heard the words, "You are no Terra." Jackson said nothing and the creature continued. Another bubble floated toward Jackson, and after it popped, he heard, "Where are you from?"

"America," Jackson said, or at least tried to say. But instead of sounds or words, a bubble came out of his mouth. It floated toward the creature and popped on its snout and then Jackson heard his voice saying, "America." With that, the two of them began to have a very slow conversation, trading words at the speed of floating bubbles.

"Never heard of it," the creature replied. "Can you fly, child of America?"

"No," Jackson said.

"I did not think so. You do not have wings. But you do not have fins either and, yet, you can fly in the ocean like a Mer. I saw you."

"We call that swimming."

"Swimming," the creature repeated. "So you are not with the Aerials?"

"No," Jackson said. "I don't even know who they are."

"And despite your ability to swimming you are not with the Mers either. Otherwise you would not be here with us."

Jackson said nothing.

"What are you doing in Dragonland?"

"One of the flying dragons took my sister. I'm here to rescue her."

"Ah, so then you and I are allies."

"Allies?"

"You are at war with the Aerials. So are we. That makes us allies. We have been at war with the Aerials and the Mers for as long as time can remember."

"Why?"

"The Mers assault our shores with their waves, and invade our land with their rivers, trying to form huge lakes in our territory that they can use as bases for their attacks. They want to cover all of Terra with their ocean. We built cliffs to protect our coasts and mountains to escape their waters. But then the Aerials joined their cause and began attacking us from the sky. They use their clouds to draw water from the oceans and dump rainfall on our land to help fill the lakes and rivers. They try to destroy our cliffs and mountains with their winds, and dump snow in our mountains to create snowcaps and glaciers so they will be inaccessible to us while also creating more rivers for the Mers. But we have ways of fighting back. We build islands to gain a foothold in the ocean, and our volcanoes can melt their snow and shoot lava rock and ash into the sky to break up their clouds."

"I saw that!" Jackson exclaimed.

"If need be, we can cover the entire sky with a thick blanket of smoke and ash that will last years. Let's hope it does not come to that. Unfortunately, we were not victorious in the last battle, and they have captured more of our land

and taken more of us prisoner. They must have believed you were one of us." The creature paused for a moment. "Although I do not see how that is possible. You look nothing like a Terra."

"Will anyone come rescue us?" Jackson asked.

The dragon became quiet and his eyes narrowed. "Terras cannot fly in the water," he said. "Only Mers can. Mers . . . and *you*."

He didn't say it, but Jackson knew what he meant. The creature was starting to suspect Jackson was a spy. And with that, their conversation ended.

12

The Curse of Dragonland

Vulture had seen some pretty baffling and horrifying things during his time as a soldier, but this was by far the most grotesque thing he had ever seen. Felton appeared to be infected by some disease or spell that was causing his body to shiver and his limbs to spasm and convulse. And yet, Felton wore a stupid-looking grin on his face as if he was enjoying it. Vulture didn't know whether to rescue Felton or slap some sense into him. After several seconds of confused, horrified silence, Vulture bellowed: "Felton, what the dragon's tail are you doing?!"

Felton froze. He looked to Campbell for help.

"It's called Dance Party," Campbell explained. "Do you want to play?"

"Felton," Vulture said with a tone that commanded, *Explain yourself.*

"The creature seems to suffer from easily-induced and intense boredom," Felton explained. "I've noticed the more time I spend with her, the worse her condition becomes."

"I know the feeling," Vulture mumbled.

"Anyway, I find she is much more talkative when playing her human games."

There was a moment of silence and Campbell noticed Vulture was looking at her funny. "It's *rude* to stare, you know."

Vulture just shook his head. "Airon wants to see you," he said to Felton. "Bring the hu—" he choked on the word, spit it out and chose another. "—creature."

A dragon tornado swept in, grabbed hold of Campbell, and pulled her out through the door and into the sky with Felton and Vulture leading the way.

Felton's lair was so far from Airon's mountain, Campbell had to fly over half of Atmos to get there. Each cloud island was like its own city, with a large mountain at the center and small cloud mountains and hills surrounding it. Airon's cloud island was atop the center of the kingdom, and it was by far the largest.

The dragon tornado swept into Airon's mountain, up the tunnel and out into the great auditorium. When Campbell arrived, Felton and Vulture were already standing before Airon. Felton was hanging his head in shame; it looked like he was being scolded.

"We only have a few days to learn anything of value from this human and you were playing games with it?!" With the seats empty, Airon's every word echoed throughout the stadium.

Felton waited for Campbell to join them before he spoke. "Your highness," he said as he raised his eyes and stepped forward. "Despite all appearances, I promise I have learned much. I have good news, and bad. The good news is the humans are not seeking an alliance with the Terras."

"And the bad?"

"Of all the histories about humans, their barbarian hordes, their knights, their kings and conquerors: from Genghis Khan to Attila the Hun to Ivan the Terrible and Vlad the Impaler—"

"Get to your point, Felton."

"The girl," he said indicating Campbell, "tells of another; one she calls Carter the Smelly Pants—"

"*Smelly* Pants?" Airon repeated. He winced with disgust as he considered why they would call someone such a thing.

Of course, this tickled Campbell to no end.

Felton continued: "To hear the girl tell of it, he is the most monstrous beast ever to walk the Earth, committing acts of unspeakable terror everywhere he goes. He can rip the head off a barbarian with his bare hands—"

"—Barbie," Campbell corrected, but Felton was on a roll.

"—he razed the Castle of Bouncy to the ground and destroyed the entire city of Lego with one kick of his leg—"

"Your point, Felton."

"It is this same Carter the Smelly Pants who has invaded our lands."

"For what purpose?"

Felton turned to Campbell. "Tell him what you told me. About Dragonsbane."

"Dragonsbane?" Airon repeated with concern.

"Ugh. It's so annoying. He just travels from one world to another hunting dragons."

"He does it for fun, Sire," Felton added. "It's a game to him. And he doesn't move on until he has slayed every dragon in the land. It is a maniacal pursuit of his; it's all he ever wants to do. And that is not the worst of it."

"Then I suggest you get to the worst of it."

"According to the human, he cannot be destroyed. Or more accurately put, even destroying him won't stop him. On one of his previous quests, he discovered something called the infinity amulet. It gives him infinite lives. So even if a dragon kills him, he can return and keep trying over and over again until he's slayed every dragon in that world."

Vulture appeared to be chewing on an idea: "Even if this Smelly Pants is the terror the creature claims—which I highly doubt—humans cannot fly. So, let the Terras deal with him. Either he is an unwitting ally in our war against them or they destroy him for us."

Vulture noticed Felton had a goofy look on his face. "What is it now, Felton? You're not going to tell us that humans can fly, too, are you?"

Felton was too embarrassed to say it, so Campbell said it for him: "On airplanes."

"An invincible human who flies around on air plains?!" Vulture huffed. "Felton, the creature is deceiving you."

"Still," Airon interjected, "He *has* escaped us twice. We dare not risk the Terras capturing him and this menace becoming one of them. Better he become an Aerial. Besides, I think I would like to see this *Carter the Smelly Pants* in action. Capture him if you can. If not, destroy him and we'll learn the truth about his *infinity amulet.*" He turned and glared at Campbell. "And continue interrogating this one while there is still time."

"Are you letting me go soon?" Campbell asked.

Airon laughed, then leaned in close. He looked Campbell over from every angle. "This is Dragonland, human. You may visit, even stay for a few nights. But stay too long and Dragonland will claim you as one of its own."

"What does that mean?!" The fear rose quickly in her belly and then exploded from her mouth with a loud burp. Only it wasn't a normal burp—all sound and smell. She could have sworn a little spurt of fire came out, too. *What the--?!* She looked to Airon in panic, hoping he would explain.

Instead, the dragon king just smiled and nodded his approval. "It could be worse," he said. He found Campbell's fear and confusion amusing. "You could have been captured by the Mers or the Terras and become one of them. This way, you will become one of the greatest dragons of all: an Aerial."

"But I don't want to be a dragon!" She turned to Felton hoping to find an ally. "They won't even let me go to school with *pink eye*. They'll never let me go back if I'm a *dragon*?!"

Airon burst out laughing. "You need not worry about that, human. You are not going anywhere. You are staying here forever."

13

Return of Carter the Smelly Pants

Carter awoke to the smell of wet ash and the sound of Bailey coughing. He bolted up—fully expecting to be in Dragonland but not at all expecting his dog to be with him. "Bailey?! What are you doing here?"

Bailey didn't answer except to growl at the surrounding trees.

"Shh. We have to be quiet," Carter said. He pet Bailey until the dog relaxed.

It was dawn and all of Dragonland was asleep . . . for now. Carter knew the dragon sun would rise soon and he didn't want to have to fight off fire-breathing dragon plants again. There was no time to waste. He checked his gear to make sure he had everything, then slipped the backpack on and slung the two paintball guns over his shoulders.

He considered the three different paths that cut through the jungle. He knew one ended at the cliff overlooking the valley. The other ended at the cliff overlooking the ocean where he and Jackson had jumped into the water and were almost eaten by a giant sea-dragon. He took the third path.

"Come on, Bailey," he said quietly. "And no barking."

They had already reached the castle-looking cliff and were halfway across the path that ran along its face when the three-headed dragon sun rose into the sky. With the dragon sun's fire lighting the entire world, Carter stopped to scan the valley and the lake below. He was hoping to see Jackson even though he knew that was a long shot. His eyes followed the river to where it split in two different directions: one that lead all the way to the mountains in the distance, and the other cut through a canyon to his left and disappeared from view. Carter knew the ocean was in that direction and so he figured the river flowed out to sea. *I bet that's where the dragon wave took Jackson?* he thought.

What to do? He could try to find Jackson. Or he could try to make it to the mountains to rescue Campbell. *All by myself.* He didn't like his options.

Furious barking broke the silence. *Bailey!* Carter realized his dog was no longer by his side. He raced through the nearest tunnel and found Bailey at the other end, barking at a tall, craggy-looking rock. He was on his haunches, hopping from side to side, preparing to attack.

"Bailey, be quiet!"

Bailey lowered his growl, but not his guard. Carter scanned their surroundings. The ground sloped upward and there were dozens—maybe hundreds—of tall rocks spread out all over the hill. A light was shining atop the hill, but it was too difficult to see where it was coming from with all the rocks in the way.

Bailey growled more loudly!

"Shh. It's just a rock, Bailey." *A hoodoo*, Carter thought, recalling the name for this type of rock that he learned in Geology class. He remembered the name because it was so funny sounding.

He walked up the path a ways to put the light at his back so he could get a better look at it. "See? Just a rock." He beckoned Bailey to him and scratched the scruff of his neck to comfort him as they looked at the rock together.

But the more Carter looked at it, the more he noticed how much the rock looked like a dragon. You had to look closely to see it, but in the crags and knobs he could see a dragon snout and dragon eyes and an open mouth with sharp dragon teeth. It looked like a disfigured dragon statue carved by a terrible sculptor.

Everything here is a dragon, Carter reminded himself.

And there wasn't just one. There were rows of them, as far as he could see, all along the path that led up the hill. *They're guarding the path*—Carter thought before noticing they were all looking up, their heads titled back, mouths open, ready to spit fire into the sky—*guarding it against the sky dragons*, he realized.

"Come on, Bailey," he said. "We're wasting time." Carter started walking back towards the tunnel when a rumbling noise erupted from the two hoodoo dragons in front of them. Bailey growled in response and reared as if getting ready to defend himself. Carter realized the hoodoo dragons were no longer looking up; they were looking down. They were looking at Bailey and him. His heart stopped.

Then came a sound like gravel being poured onto a sidewalk and the hoodoo dragon's mouth began to glow red. "Baily, run!"

Carter and Bailey sprinted up the path just as the two hoodoo dragons spewed molten lava out of their mouths like volcanic vomit. It melted the ground where Carter and Bailey had stood only a second before.

The rumbling noise was repeated a dozen times over again, so loud it filled the sky. All of the hoodoo dragons along the path were moving their heads and aiming their red glowing mouths at Carter and Bailey. Carter stopped short just as two more streams of lava spewed from the two hoodoo dragons in front of him. Their mouths sizzled and smoked with lava drool.

Carter heard the gravel sound behind them. "This way!" he shouted, and he and Bailey ran to the side and then up the path, dodging the stream of lava vomit behind them. *It's like a video game*, Carter thought as he tried to settle his nerves. *I just need to figure out how to pass this level.*

He scanned the scene. The hoodoo dragons were spaced out in such a way, and turned their heads so slowly, that he could escape their lava vomit by zigzagging up the slope.

"Wait," he said, as much to himself as to Bailey. The hoodoo dragons turned their heads and aimed their red glowing mouths at him. Still, he waited until he heard the gravel sound. "Now!" He ran up the slope as fast as he could, zigging and zagging between the hoodoo dragons every time he heard one make the gravel sound. Streams of lava crossed the air behind him and he felt the intense heat on his neck. Smoke filled the air.

And then he stopped short. In front of him, just beyond the last row of hoodoo dragons, a giant diamond castle grew out of the top of the hill. It had slanted diamond walls with diamond towers at the edges, and a large diamond archway in the center that opened into a hallway. It seemed to glow in the sunlight.

Holy cow, Carter thought, realizing this must have been the explosion of light he saw from the sky yesterday. The gravel sound came again, and he ran as fast as he could for the entrance when he noticed something was moving inside. It was difficult to see through the diamond walls, but something was coming out. He turned sharply to his right, dodging another lava stream, and sprinted several hundred feet away from the entrance and crouched behind the nearest hoodoo dragon. Intense heat came off the rock. He grabbed Bailey by the collar to hold him in check.

Carter peeked out toward the castle just in time to see three tiger dragons emerge. They looked as if they were expecting an attack from the sky and were confused to find nothing above them. They noticed the dragon rocks were all looking down which seemed to confuse them even more. One spotted a puddle of smoldering lava and burning dirt and walked toward it, its head in a swivel. The others split up and started down different paths.

"Shh," Carter said quietly to Bailey.

Once at the lava puddle, the tiger dragon sniffed the ground. Then it sniffed the air. It called out to the others; it had caught wind of something.

I think one of us needs a bath, Bailey? Carter thought, realizing they had been discovered.

All three of the tiger dragons were headed in his direction. He edged his way around the hoodoo dragon to stay out of sight, trying to think of what to do, how to escape. And then, he heard the rumble. He looked up to find the hoodoo dragon was staring down at him, its mouth afire.

Carter grabbed his paintball gun and shot several pellets down the path in the opposite direction. The tiger dragons heard the splats and rushed to investigate. The gravel sound made its way up the hoodoo dragon, like rocks rattling in a pipe. Carter and Bailey sprinted for the castle just as lava rained down from the hoodoo dragon's glowing hot mouth, burning the ground where they had stood a mere second before.

The tiger dragons were surveying the paint splats, mystified to find it wasn't lava, when they heard the latest vomit. They raced for the hoodoo dragon where seconds ago Carter had been hiding. They could still smell him.

Carter raced down the main hallway of the diamond castle only to realize Bailey had stopped following him. Instead, the dog stood at the entrance to a smaller hallway, waiting for Carter.

"That's a dead end, Bailey," Carter said as he examined the hallway. "We need to go this way." Carter took a few steps down the main hallway, but Bailey didn't budge. "Bailey. Come on."

Bailey waved his head one more time, and then started down the small hallway.

"Bailey," Carter whisper-shouted. Carter may have been arguing with Bailey, but Bailey wasn't arguing with him. Carter gave up and followed his dog—and lucky for him! Because only a second later the three tiger-dragons went racing up the main hallway.

"Good boy," Carter said as he scratched Bailey behind the ears. He peeked down the main hallway, consulted with Bailey to make sure they were in agreement, then followed the tiger dragons.

The hallway led into a giant opening that looked equal parts cave and football stadium. The walls were made of thick rock with layer upon layer of ledges that rose about halfway up like stadium seating. From there, the rock was replaced by large crystals that stretched and curved to form a dome ceiling. Light rained down from above and, as it passed through the crystal ceiling, it splintered off into a thousand directions and colors. It felt like being inside a kaleidoscope. Carter and Bailey crouched down into a corner and watched as hundreds of dragons filed in, taking their spots along the rock ledges. All eyes were on a much larger dragon that stood alone on a larger, more ornate-looking ledge at the head of the cave. Whereas most of the other dragons resembled animals, this one looked a lot like the dragon statues Carter's father brought back from China—the kind without wings. He had a long, windy body covered in spikes, four long legs that ended in vicious claws, and a long tail that ended in what looked like a medieval weapon. Carter guessed he was their king.

". . . Wait for the earthquake and volcanic eruptions," the dragon king was saying. "Then we'll use the lava tubes to rescue them."

As the three tiger dragons made their way into the cave, the crowd stepped aside so they could approach the king. They were unable to find the intruders, they reported.

"It could be a trap," a lion dragon said. "They might be waiting for us to leave Terra unguarded so they can invade. We should not leave before finding the intruders."

"It's more likely the intruders are spies sent here to discover our plan," the king said. "If we wait, we give them time to warn the others. We *must* attack now."

With that, the king led them through a side hallway where they all disappeared. Carter and Bailey followed, being sure to stay out of sight—and out of smelling distance.

The hallway slanted downward and when they finally caught up to the dragons, they found them gathered in a large underground cavern, waiting at the mouth of a tunnel. Pointy rock formations hung glowing from the ceiling.

Stala . . . something, Carter thought, trying to remember what they were called. He had studied these in Geology class too. *Maybe mom has a point. Maybe I should study more,* he admitted as he gave up trying to remember the name.

He turned his attention from the spiky rocks back to the dragons; they hadn't moved. *What are they waiting for?* Carter wondered.

Then the ground shook and a giant commotion roared in the distance. It lasted for almost a minute before everything became still again.

"Now!" the king shouted and led his dragon army charging down the tunnel.

Carter waited a beat before following. "Come on, Bailey," he said finally, and they entered the tunnel. The tunnel was too dark to see anything, so Carter turned on his flashlight, being careful to point it down at his feet so as to not attract too much attention. The rock had changed color and texture—it even smelled different. "We must be in the lava tubes," Carter said, even though he had no way of knowing what a lava tube smelled like.

They continued following the dragons, staying at a safe distance, until Bailey veered off into a smaller lava tube that branched off from the main one.

Carter paused. "They went this way," he said, pointing down the main lava tube.

This time Bailey didn't argue with him; he didn't even turn around. He just quickened his pace and continued down the smaller lava tube. Carter jogged after him, thinking, *I hope you know where you're going, Bailey*.

14

The Rescue

Jackson tried not to stare, but he didn't want to look away, either. The captured dragon was clearly glaring at him, and—cell or not—Jackson felt he needed to keep up his guard. When the creature spoke again, the bubble didn't flow over to Jackson; it drifted upward to another dragon locked in the cell above him—a bear dragon. The bubble popped on the bear dragon's face, but the sound was too faint for Jackson to hear. Then the bear dragon said something and a bubble sank down past Jackson to another dragon locked in a cell beneath him. Jackson realized the cells were stacked. There were literally dozens if not hundreds of dragons all around him. And each one was eying *him*.

The bear dragon gave Jackson a long mean look, then said something to the dragon opposite him. Two bubbles came out of its snout and were floating through the water when a rumble shook the sea. The air bubbles started to sway and bounce violently until they were carried over to Jackson and one popped on his face. "I saw him trying to sneak into Terra when the attack came," it said. The other bubble was about to float away when Jackson reached out and popped it. "He's a spy."

The rumble grew and the water tossed more violently. The ground slid out from under the coral prison and large sections of coral broke apart and collapsed. Scratchy howls echoed throughout the water as the coral claws tried to grab onto each other and hold themselves together, but it was no use. The entire coral prison was crumbling.

Jackson looked up, expecting the bear dragon to pounce on him, but he seemed as shocked and confused as Jackson was. *Now's my chance*, Jackson thought. He kicked with all his might. The coral claws grabbed hold of him and tried to hold him back, but he ripped them apart from the rest of the coral prison. They hung limply from Jackson's clothes until they eventually just let go and floated away.

Jackson tried to swim for the surface, but the turbulence in the water was carrying him back toward the prison—toward the bear dragon. The bear dragon realized this too and waited for him with an angry snarl. Jackson flipped in the water and dove down, just narrowly escaping the bear dragon's claws.

The bear dragon was about to give chase when an army of dragon currents flew through the water like a hurricane, trying to wrangle all the prisoners.

Jackson looked back just as one grabbed hold of the bear dragon. He didn't have any time to waste. He swam along the bottom, trying to stay clear of the chaos, then he pressed off the ocean floor and shot for the surface only to stop himself short—a blanket of seaweed dragons were floating above him, waiting. He let himself sink and eyed the surface, looking for a clearing. He looked back toward the coral dungeon. Out of the chaos of currents and coral and disrupted sand came two dragon currents headed for him with such speed he had no chance of out-swimming them.

There was another loud rumble and an eruption of volcanic ash shot upward, tearing through the water right past him and blowing a hole through the blanket of seaweed.

Around the eruption, Jackson could see an island growing out of the sea floor and rising to the surface. That was his way out! He swam towards the eruption and was blasted to the surface on the upward stream of volcanic ash.

Jackson crawled his way onto a newly-formed island and sat down to catch his breath. The island wasn't very big—about size of his bedroom. All around him, several other smalls islands were forming in the ocean and Terras were running up their slopes.

Now what? Jackson wondered. The shore was too far away to swim for safety—even if he didn't have to worry about merdragons and dragon currents chasing him. And he *did* have to worry about them.

A dragon wave repeatedly attacked his island and, with each onslaught, grabbed the island's sandy ash in its water claws and dragged it out to sea. It wouldn't be long before it eroded the entire island.

With its next attack, the dragon wave crashed onto Jackson's legs and tried to drag him out to sea. Jackson held on but, as the wave receded, a seaweed dragon wrapped itself around his legs and tied them together. He tried to climb further up the island, but the ashy sand was so loose, it was difficult to pull himself up. Another dragon wave crashed onto Jackson's legs and, together with the seaweed dragon, pulled him toward the sea.

Jackson dug his hands into the island, trying to hold on, but he just pulled mounds of sand with him instead. He was certain he would be recaptured when he heard barking. It sounded a lot like a dog—*his* dog! *Bailey?!* He looked up toward the sound, but instead of Bailey he saw Carter standing at the top of the island.

"Jackson!"

What the—how? Jackson was befuddled. *How did Carter get here? And why was he dressed to go skateboarding?*

Bailey ran up next to Carter and barked more loudly than before. Carter reached forward and grabbed Jackson by the hand, and with Carter's help, Jackson pulled himself further up the island. The dragon-seaweed, realizing it was being dragged onto land, unwrapped itself from Jackson's legs and tried to slide back into the sea when Bailey grabbed it in his jaws. He dragged it ashore and shook it furiously until it had stopped squirming.

"How did you get here?" Jackson asked.

"I'll explain later," Carter said. "Here." He pulled a pair of Jackson's shoes out of his backpack and handed them to his brother. "What happened to your face?" he asked as he watched Jackson tie them on.

"What do you mean?"

"You look . . . *fishy*."

"Stop goofing around, Carter. We have to get out of here before they tear this island apart!"

Carter didn't bother arguing with him. What was the use without a mirror? But there was no doubt Jackson had the beginnings of a fish face.

"Come on," Carter said. He led the way down a hole in the island, which turned out to be the top of an underwater volcano. As they climbed further down into the crater, they heard the dragon waves lashing against its walls. "This way," Carter said as he and Bailey crawled down into a tunnel.

"Where are we?"

"Lava tube. It'll take us all the way back to land." Carter handed Jackson a paintball gun.

What the heck am I supposed to do with this? Jackson thought. "And why is Bailey here?" he added aloud as their dog led the way down the lava tube. "Did you feed him dragon fruit?"

"I think he crawled into my bed. I must have brought him with me same as the paintball guns." Carter wrinkled his brow as he tried to make sense of it all. "How come you didn't wake up when I did?" he asked.

"I don't know. Weren't you captured, too?"

"I was, but then the dragon that was carrying me dropped me. I was about to smack into the ground when I woke up."

"That must be it. I didn't wake up because I was still captured. That would explain why Campbell didn't wake up either. You woke up before you hit the ground, just like you would in a nightmare. And we woke up when the sea serpent was about to eat us. So, I don't think we have to worry about dying here because we'll wake up first. But we cannot get captured."

As they continued down the lava tube, Jackson explained everything he had learned. There are three types of dragons: Aerials, Mers and Terras, and the Terras are fighting a war against the other two. "They thought I was a spy," he said. "The dragons that took Campbell might believe the same thing about her."

Jackson was about to exit into a much larger lava tube, when Carter grabbed him by the shirt and pulled him back.

"That way leads back to the Terra castle," he said.

As soon as he said it, they heard the rumble of footsteps approaching from down the large lava tube. Carter turned off his flashlight and they stepped back into their tunnel and up against the wall just as a stampede of Terras stormed by. They couldn't see them in the dark, but they felt the ground shake as they passed.

"If we can't go that way, how do we get out of here?" Jackson whispered.

Carter furled his brow and tried to think it through. "Let's wait for them to all to leave first and then—" he started to say but stopped short when he felt something cold flowing over his feet. It was too dark to see what it was, so he stomped his foot a few times. They heard splashing.

"Water?"

"Where is it coming from?"

"Uh-oh," Jackson said with realization.

"What?"

"The water dragons were trying to erode the walls of the crater."

"So?"

"So, once the crater's walls are gone, the ocean will flood into it." More water raced into the lava tube. "We can't stay here much longer. Are they gone?"

Carter flashed his light into the larger lava tube and it landed on the bear dragon; it was glaring right at them, rearing on its haunches, ready to pounce.

The boys thought they were goners for sure when, just as the dragon bear was about to leap for them, the ground shook violently.

"Another earthquake!" Jackson yelled as the walls of the lava tube groaned and rocks began falling from above.

"They must be trying to block the tunnel." Carter said. "To keep the water out."

The dragon bear stepped back just in time to dodge a rock from striking its head. It roared in frustration and gave the boys an angry look that promised they'd meet again just as a giant slab of the ceiling caved in, blocking the bear dragon from view. The fallen slab created a ramp up to the surface. Black, gravelly sand flowed down the incline. Bailey raced up to the surface and the boys followed.

They found themselves on a black sand beach that was almost completely walled in by tall gray cliffs. The only break in the cliff wall was at the other end of the beach, about a hundred yards away. But about fifty yards between them and escape, the Terras were climbing out from another hole.

The boys backed away slowly, hoping that in all of the chaos they would go unnoticed.

To their relief, the Terras were not hanging around. A few stayed to help their comrades to the surface, but the rest raced off toward their castle.

The boys started to relax, believing they were safe, when the bear dragon crawled out of the hole. He immediately turned in their direction and, upon spotting them, let out a vicious roar and raced towards them. He couldn't fly—he had no wings—but he ran with such speed he might as well have been flying. The boys stood frozen: an ocean to their right, cliffs to their left and rear, and a bear dragon in front of them. There was no escape.

Carter took his paint gun off his shoulder and aimed it at the charging bear dragon.

"What are you going to do with *that*?!" Jackson shouted.

Hopefully blind him, Carter thought. The ground rumbled as the creature approached. Bailey reared on his haunches and barked furiously, warning the bear dragon to stay back. But it continued to charge. It leapt over Bailey, its jaws and claws hungry to tear into Carter. Carter rapid fired his paint gun and several paint pellets splattered all over the creature's face. Carter dove off to the side, leaving the bear dragon to crash chin first into the black sand.

The boys backed away toward the cliffs as the creature howled, then growled, and shook its head furiously trying to clear the paint from its eyes. It was clear from its pained expression that the paint stung and it was having problems seeing. But eventually it *could* see again. And after scanning the beach it found them. The boys stood several feet apart, guns aimed and waited.

The bear dragon set its eyes on Jackson and raced for him. Jackson fired, but missed. Bailey, by his side, barked anxiously as if to cheer him on. Jackson fired again, but the creature swayed its head to dodge the pellet. Jackson fired again just as the bear dragon leapt for him and the paint splattered harmlessly off its chest. Jackson continued firing as the creature's shadow engulfed him. Its claws were only inches from his face when a stream of water burst from the ground beneath the creature and thrust it into the air.

A geyser! Jackson realized, although it wasn't like any geyser he had seen before. Whatever it was, it was definitely water and Jackson knew by now to fear the *water* in Dragonland just as much as the *dragons*. He instinctively stepped back. And sure enough, after the water disappeared back into its hole, the bear dragon was gone.

"Holy cow!" Carter shouted. "It was like the water *grabbed* him."

Carter's words were still running through Jackson's mind when another geyser shot up from the ground—this one right behind them.

As it rose into the air, the water looked like two giant claws reaching for the sky. Jackson pulled his little brother away just as the water claws splashed down on the ground— the ground where only a second before Carter had stood— and dragged the surrounding black sand down into the hole.

The ground rumbled with such intensity they almost lost their footing. Bailey growled at the gravel sand. Another geyser shot into the air, then another and another until they were surrounded by explosions of water rising into the air and water claws grasping for their heads.

"We have to get away from the coast!" Jackson shouted.

Bailey took off running towards the distant cliffs, when a stream of water burst through the ground beneath him and sent him twirling and howling twenty feet into the air."

"Bailey!" Carter shouted. But after the water claws slipped back into the hole, Bailey was nowhere to be seen.

His howls still echoed in the air. "What happened to him?" Carter asked, looking down the geyser hole. "Did they get him?"

"Carter, be careful," Jackson said as he yanked his brother away from the hole. The ground was vibrating. "We have to get out of here."

"We have to go after him!"

"If we stay here, they're going to get us, too!"

He grabbed Carter by the arm and dragged him away just as another rush of water exploded from the geyser hole, its water claws narrowly missing Carter's heels.

They zigged and zagged their way toward the cliff, using the underground vibrations to predict where the geysers were going to erupt next. But they were running out of beach. Soon they would be pinned against the cliff with nowhere else to go.

How far away from the ocean do we need to go to escape these things! Carter wondered. As he neared the cliff face, he realized it wasn't sheer, but was made up of block-shaped rocks that looked like building blocks stacked on top of each other. The rocks formed a natural staircase that made it easy for the boys to climb up.

They zigged and zagged their way up the rock steps, dodging the water claws that scratched against the cliff hoping to grab hold of them, until the boys finally pulled themselves over the top. A line of geysers shot up along the cliff. The water claws were still reaching for them, but they were too high up. They were safe.

They rested to catch their breath and looked out on the scene they had just escaped. Off in the distance, it looked like a battlefield only with streams of water blasting up into the sky instead of bombs raining down. A geyser shot into the air and, on its way down, grabbed a nearby Terra. The creature screamed in terror as the water claws dragged it down the geyser hole and drowned its screams under sand and water.

"Bailey," Carter said with regret and sadness. A heavy silence hung in the air for several seconds.

Jackson rose to his feet and looked toward the giant mountain in the distance. He turned back to the battle that was still raging on the beach and let out a frustrated sigh. He didn't have to say it for Carter to understand what he was thinking: Go back for Bailey or onward to save Campbell?

"You know, I didn't actually see him go under," Jackson said. "Maybe he woke up before it grabbed him."

"Promise me if they *do* have him, we'll come back for him."

"Of course."

An expression of stubborn resolve came across Carter's face as he rose to his feet. Without saying another word, they marched in the direction of the giant mountain, determined to save their little sister.

15

Home or Dragon

When Campbell returned to Felton's lair, she grabbed her stuffed panda bear and gave it a long hard squeeze. "I like hugs," it replied. But not in the same cute voice she heard before. This voice was more gruff. Only then did she notice the stuffed animal looked different. Less like a stuffed bear and more like a stuffed . . . *dragon!?*

Eventually everything in Dragonland becomes a dragon, Airon had warned her. Even without a mirror, she knew *she* was turning into a dragon, too. She could foresee her fate in the stuffed animal's transformation.

Campbell became electric with frantic energy; she felt tingly as if her whole body was being shocked into action. But this wasn't fear. There was no room in her mind for fear. This was more like the last thirty seconds in Dance Party when she needed to execute the perfect dance move to win. This was urgency, a time to focus.

Campbell knew the way out of Felton's lair. That wasn't the problem. The problem was, unlike a human door that was on the ground, his dragon door was halfway up the wall. *Can I jump that high?* She wondered as she stared up at the wispy layer of clouds covering the hole.

"What are you doing?" Felton asked from his desk. He was so distracted, she hoped he wasn't paying any attention to her.

"I'm bored. What are you reading?"

"The diary we captured from the human invaders."

"What does it say?"

He read a passage: "'. . . By the fourth day, we barely recognized ourselves. We appeared to be transforming into dragons more and more with each day. But those who returned before nightfall remained unaffected. We suspect there's some sort of spell in this land, and if we stay too long, we become one of them. It's a clever form of defense.'"

"Does it say how they got back?" she asked hesitantly, afraid the question might give away her plan.

But Felton didn't even hear her. He was entranced by something in the book. Campbell looked over his shoulder at a drawing of what looked half man, half dragon. "He kind of looks like you, Felton."

Felton must have already been thinking the same thing. He remained eerily quiet.

"Felton? Felton, what's wrong?"

"I don't want to talk about it."

"Do you think that really *is* you?"

"No." He shook his head as if he was wrestling with the thought. "I mean, true, I have never felt like I belonged here. But I don't remember being human. Wouldn't I remember? Or is that what Airon meant when he said I only had a few days with which to question you? Because after you become a dragon, you forget about being human."

The thought spooked Campbell. Not only might she turn into a dragon, but she might forget everything about herself? Her life would be *erased*, like it never happened? She needed to escape and now!

"I know!" she shouted excitedly. "Let's resume your lessons. Maybe learning more about humans will help you remember."

"I'm not in the mood to learn anything."

"Well, we can't have you just moping around all day. We'll play hide and seek!"

"What's hide and seek?"

"Oh, Felton, you'll love it. It's so much fun! And if you ever *were* a human child you almost certainly would have played it. You might remember it."

"I guess."

"Okay, close your eyes and count to a hundred—no, a thousand. While you're counting, I'll go hide. And then you have to find me."

"Whatever." He continued staring at the drawing in the book.

"Don't be like Carter. Now, close your eyes."

He continued to stare. She closed the book and took it from him. "Close your eyes."

He finally did.

"Okay, now start counting to a million."

She waited for him to start counting, and then she quietly tiptoed toward the exit, book in hand.

Here goes nothing. She jumped with all her might and sprung so high into the air that, if she didn't know better, she would have sworn she was flying. She sailed right through the hole and landed outside.

I guess sometimes you don't know what you're capable of until you try.

The area around Felton's cloud hill was desolate. His was the only hill around, and there were no other clouds in the sky. It was lonely out here and she started to feel sorry for Felton. The other dragons didn't seem to treat him very well. Even his cloud hill wasn't much of a hill. It was more of a mound. A small cloud mound out in the middle of nowhere. But all that was to her advantage; she was trying to escape after all.

Campbell looked up in the sky and found where Airon's giant cloud mountain towered in the distance. Instinctively, she turned and started off in the opposite direction.

16

Onward

The dragon sun was high in the sky by the time the boys reached the opposite end of the cliff. From there, the ground gradually sloped down into a barren valley. As they hiked down, the terrain became rocky and uneven with sharp loose rocks jutting out here and there. Each step was a potential hazard. Jackson was thinking how painful it would be to hike barefoot, when he turned to his brother and said, "Thanks for the shoes."

Carter just nodded. He kept his eyes on the ground to watch his footing and make sure he didn't take a wrong step on a shard of rock and turn his ankle, or slip and go sliding all the way down to the bottom. When he finally reached level ground, he paused to look out at the giant mountain in the distance. They had been walking for what felt like an hour and they still seemed no closer to it. It was depressing.

At the valley floor, the rocky terrain gave way to a dry and cracked yellow desert. Miles of it—dry, harsh terrain. But at least here the going was less treacherous and since he no longer needed to concentrate on where he stepped, Jackson made conversation.

"So, you told mom about Dragonland and she agreed to take you shopping to buy *weapons*?" Jackson asked. "That doesn't sound like mom."

"Well, not at first. At first she sent me to my room."

"Okay, *that* sounds like mom."

Carter chuckled when he felt something mushy under his shoe. "What the—?" He looked back and noticed he had squashed a small mound of sand. He was about to walk on when he felt a sharp burning pain on his calf. "Ow!" he shouted and reflectively smacked at his leg.

"What's the matter?"

"Something bit me." Cater inspected his calf and noticed his skin was smoking—actually smoking! "What the—!? Something *burned* me!"

From the mound came a swarm of what looked like ants. With furious speed they crawled up Carter's shoes and legs, spitting out tiny flames along their way.

"Ow!" Carter shouted, swiping at his legs. "Dragon ants!"

"Watch out!"

Carter looked up to see Jackson aiming his paintball gun at him.

"What are you—?"

Jackson pulled the trigger rapid fire and a flurry of paint balls flew out and exploded against Carter's legs.

"Ow! That hurt!"

"Worse than the dragon ants?" Jackson walked toward the ant hill, firing the entire time until the whole mound was covered in paint. He paused to make sure he had beat back the attack when—splat. "Ow!"

Carter had shot him. "You had a dragon ant on you." Jackson just looked at him with an angry frown. "You should thank me," Carter continued. "I saved you."

"Yeah, right." Jackson gave a second look at the ant hill before moving on. "Be on the lookout for more of those—" he started to say before stopping short. "Uh-oh."

Only then did they realize there were thousands of mounds all around them. And from each one erupted a swarm of dragon ants.

"What do we do?"

"Dragons or not, they're still the size of ants. We can outrun them," Jackson said, before adding with doubt: "Right?"

The ground all around them had turned a throbbing red mess. "Outrun them where? They have us surrounded."

"Follow my lead." There was only one option: pick out the weakest point and charge. Jackson replaced his paintball canister with a full load and aimed his gun at the line of dragon ants approaching from the front. "When I say go, fire a path for us to break through. Got it?"

Carter nodded.

They walked calmly but with purpose. The swarm was getting closer. Twenty yards away. Ten yards. Carter looked to his brother: "Now?"

But Jackson just shook his head and continued on. Five yards. Three.

"Now!" Jackson fired, carving a painted path through the dragon ants. They made it several hundred yards before their paint pellets ran out and they needed to switch cannisters. After reloading, they continued on for a few hundred more yards, but their ammo was running low. They stopped to reload again—their last cannisters—when Jackson noticed the ants were no longer closing in. They had the boys encircled, but they were holding their positions instead of approaching further. It was a stalemate.

Jackson checked their distance from the mountain range. "I'm not sure we have enough paintballs to make it," he said. The boys stayed on alert, but held their fire as they tried to figure out their next move. The dragon ants, for their part, seemed to have changed tactics too—opting to keep the boys trapped instead of swarming them. *But why?*

"What are they doing?" Carter wondered.

Then the ground began to shake. They saw the cloud of dust before they saw the creatures themselves. Hundreds of Terras charging their way.

"Waiting for reinforcements!" Jackson said.

As the stampede charged towards them, the dragons ants dispersed, *So they won't get trampled with us*, Jackson reasoned.

"Run!"

The boys took off. Jackson kept looking over his shoulder to see the Terras closing in on them. Two smaller groups split off from the main herd—one to each side. There was a cliff in front of them, and if the Terras made it the cliff before the boys, they'd have them trapped. "They're trying to cut us off," he said.

Carter looked over his shoulder to see the ground crumble beneath one of the Terras and the creature fell into—*Is that water?* He wondered.

The fallen creature tried to climb back up, but the ground kept crumbling away beneath it. The other Terras screeched to a halt. Just as the fallen Terra was about to make it back onto land, two long tentacles grabbed it and dragged it under water.

"Jackson, look!" Carter shouted.

The ground beneath the Terras was cracking like thin ice, and they were afraid to come closer. They stared at the boys in angry frustration. The ground gave way beneath another Terra and it fell into the water. It let out a panicked shriek and tried to climb back to safety, but in its panic, it just caused more of the ground to crack and break away.

"Uh oh," Carter said. A crack was headed right for them like a slow-motion bolt of lightning drawn on sand. And then, the ground all around them began to crack into a thousand pieces like sheets of ice, revealing a large lake underneath.

The boys each found themselves on their own small sheet of land. They dropped to their knees, palms flat on the ground, as their sheets bobbed up and down violently like boogie boards in the ocean.

"Something just passed underneath us," Jackson said.

The Terras were too heavy for the land sheets and many of them tipped over and fell into the water. They struggled in panic to get back on top. The scene became absolute chaos—furious splashes, lashing tentacles and desperate screams as, one by one, the Terras were dragged underwater.

Carter looked for an escape. "There's a ledge!" he shouted with a nod toward the cliff, and the boys—no strangers to paddling through waves—dropped to their stomachs and paddled with all their might.

Jackson got there first and, as his land sheet approached the ledge, he rose to a knee, waited until his sheet smashed against the ledge, and then rolled safely onto land.

He turned and saw something underwater was chasing his brother. "Hurry, Carter!"

A tentacle reached out from underwater and was just about to grab Carter by the neck when the ground around the lake shook violently. Huge shock waves rippled through the water. One wave swept the creature away in one direction and another wave picked up Carter and sent him surfing toward Jackson. Carter rose to one knee and waited, and just before his land sheet crashed into edge of the lake, shattering into a thousand pieces, he pushed off and tumbled safely onto the ledge.

"Are you okay," Jackson asked as he helped his brother to his feet.

Carter nodded. After he regained his senses, he asked: "What's happening to the lake?"

The water level was going down, almost like water draining from a bathtub. In seconds all the water was gone and dozens of Mers—shark dragons and giant squid dragons that were still holding Terras in their tentacles—were left flopping helplessly on the dry bottom. The tables had turned and the Terras—rhino dragons and tiger dragons and bear dragons—pounced on the Mers, freeing their friends and taking their enemies prisoner.

The sound of splashing water filled the air as river water jumped over the edge of the dry lake like a waterfall, trying with all its might to refill the lake and give the Mers a fighting chance. The water rose quickly, providing enough water for the Mers to swim in, enabling them to fight back. They were about to gain the upper hand when the ground shook violently again.

Another earthquake, Carter thought. A huge gash split the cliff in two. "Look out," he shouted, pulling his brother away just as lava spewed out through the crack and into the lakebed. The water screamed and hissed, evaporating into steam as the lava hit it. Soon, the entire lakebed was covered in steam and Jackson and Carter could see nothing through the mist. But they could still hear the grunts and pained cries of a fierce battle below.

"Let's get out of here," Jackson said. They raced along the ledge—the cliff on one side, the river on the other, the cries of battle fading behind them.

In the distance ahead stood the highest mountain, its peak covered in snow. The snow cap looked like a giant white claw that had grabbed the mountain by its head and was trying to push it back down into the ground. From its white claws ran little streams of water that flowed down the mountain and collected into the very river the boys were walking along. As they walked, the mountain's shadow slowly crept over them and darkened the mood. They slowed their pace.

Carter spotted two dragon waves in the river, racing back and forth. They reminded him of guard dogs running back and forth along a chain link fence. "They're following us," he said.

"Who?"

Carter just nodded to the dragon waves. One turned toward them and threw itself against the riverbank, like a guard dog jumping against a fence. The other followed its lead and was able to reach higher—almost onto the ledge.

More dragon waves appeared and stalked the boys like angry dogs, occasionally throwing themselves against the riverbank ferociously. Their splashes sounded more like growls and howls than crashing waves and the river boiled with their fury.

Without exchanging a word, the boys turned their walk into a jog. They heard the commotion coming from the river, but they kept their eyes on the path ahead. The mountain towered above them; they were almost there. And then a wave swept across the ledge and slammed Carter into the side of the cliff. He fell down on his back and began sliding toward the river as if the water was a conveyor belt carrying him away.

Jackson dove and grabbed Carter just before he fell over the edge and into the river.

"Are you okay?!"

Carter was still dazed, but eventually he regained his senses and nodded.

"Come on!" Jackson said, helping his brother to his feet. They took off in a full sprint for the mountain—keeping one eye on the path and the other on the waves. Now and again, they would stop short to dodge a dragon wave, and then take off at full sprint again to dodge another. Their sides ached and their legs cramped, but they powered their way up the mountain slope until they rose above the cliff that walled in the path and they were free to put more distance between themselves and the river.

Once safe, Carter collapsed to his knees and tried to catch his breath. Jackson, with his hands on his hips and his heart pounding, looked toward the top of the mountain. Thick spines ran down from the top with deep gullies in between. The river they had just escaped started at the snow cap and flowed down one of the ravines in the mountainside. Water could just as easily flow down any of the others.

"We should stick to ridges," Jackson said. "Ready?" He offered a hand to Carter, but Carter stayed seated. "Maybe if you were more active and didn't sit around playing video games all day," Jackson said with a smile.

"Okay, *mom*."

"Seriously, come on. We've got to get out of this ravine. They can send water down it at any moment."

Carter didn't even hear the end of the sentence. All he heard was the roar of rushing water. He grabbed Jackson's hand and hopped up to his feet. They raced up the side of the ravine; its slope was so steep that they needed to crawl up it on their hands and feet. By the time they reached the top, water was flowing down the ravine on other side of the ridge, too. They were trapped, boxed in by two rivers, and the water was rising fast. Soon it would wash over the ridge.

"Come on!"

They raced along the spine towards the mountaintop. Carter's thighs burned and ached; his side was cramping, and each breath felt like a shot of fire through his lungs. But there was no stopping. He could already feel the occasional splash of angry water on his legs, and they were only halfway up the mountain. *We're not going to make it,* he was thinking when Jackson shouted:

"There's a cave!"

They were less than a hundred feet from safety when the ground shook violently and there was a thunderous roar of rumbles and crashes.

"Rockslide!"

Large boulders charged down the mountain like an angry herd. Jackson slid to the side to dodge one, and then jumped over another. Carter jumped over one boulder and then ducked before another almost took off his head. His legs were growing weak and when he tried to jump over another rock, he couldn't get high enough and the boulder took out his legs. He crashed into the ground and looked up just as another boulder was about to smash him in the face. He rolled over, just narrowly dodging it. And then all went quiet.

They rose to their feet, dusted themselves off, and surveyed the fallout. The good news: the boulders had filled in the ravines and forced the rivers to change course. So the boys were now safe from the water. The bad news: the boulders had also walled off the entrance to the cave.

"*Now* what?" Carter said.

"There's a space at the top. Maybe we can climb through it." Jackson sat down on a boulder that had settled a few feet away. "Just give me a sec."

"Maybe *you* should be more active."

Jackson offered a weak smile, but noticed his brother wasn't laughing. In fact, his brother looked freaked out. "Jackson, get up."

"Okay, *mom*," Jackson said in jest.

"I'm not joking." Carter drew his paintball gun and aimed it at the boulder Jackson was sitting on.

Jackson looked down to see two angry eyes glaring up at him. He rose and looked at the rock wall blocking the entrance to the cave. So many boulders. And they all had eyes—angry eyes—glaring at them, threatening to smash them if they tried to enter the cave. He surveyed the top of the mountain: it was littered with a thousand angry-eyed boulders, all glaring at the boys and awaiting their next move.

"I still think the cave is our best bet," Jackson said as he studied the wall of boulders blocking the entrance. "It doesn't look like the boulders have claws or anything like that."

"Do they have *mouths*?" Carter asked. "Because the hoodoo dragons guarding their castle had mouths and they could spit *lava*."

Jackson shook his head. "I think they would have tried that by now if they could."

"Yeah, well, they can still smash us."

That gave Jackson an idea. "How many paintballs do you have left?"

"Less than half a cannister."

Jackson counted the boulders. "Twenty should do it. Take out their eyes." He pulled his paintball gun and approached the wall.

Carter watched as his brother fired methodically, blinding the boulders one by one. He waited until Jackson said, "I'm out," before taking his turn to blind the rest of the rocks.

After Carter emptied his ammo, Jackson put his finger to his lips to signal for Carter to stay quiet. Jackson whispered in his ear, "The minute we try to climb through, they'll crash on top of us. We have to bait them. Wait over there." He pointed to the side of the cave entrance.

Carter watched as Jackson played it out in his mind. He nodded to the rhythm of a song only he could hear, psyching himself up. He sprinted for the wall, jumped and placed his foot on a painted boulder midway up, launched himself up toward the top, but then pushed off with his hands, back and to the side. He landed next to Carter by the side of the entrance. The blinded boulders shook loose and tumbled, hoping to crush whoever was trying to climb them, but they tumbled harmlessly down the mountain instead.

The mountain shook again and they heard the rumble of boulders above tumbling toward them. Jackson and Carter rushed inside the cave and looked back just in time to see another rockslide go charging past the cave entrance. The boulders were too late; the boys were safe inside.

The cave was actually the entrance to a lava tube that ran deep into a volcano. At the other end, it opened onto a spiral path that circled the inner wall of the volcano, leading all the way up to the top. At the bottom, there was a lake of boiling lava. They could feel its heat.

The boys continued towards the top, slowly, uneasily, their heads in a swivel. Everything in this world was a potential hazard. Carter half expected the volcano to contract like a throat and swallow them.

Near the top, a row of smaller holes circled the inner rim of the volcano. "These are kind of like the holes forts have for cannons," Jackson said. "Only these holes angle up."

Carter looked out through one of the holes. "They're aimed towards that wall of clouds." He turned and surveyed the inside of the volcano. It reminded him of the cave beneath the Terra's crystal castle. "I don't think this is where the dragon brought Campbell," he said.

"It was headed for this mountain."

"That doesn't mean it stopped here." Carter looked through the cannon hole again towards the large wall of clouds. "The land dragons live on land, seas dragons in the sea. It only makes sense that the sky dragons would live—"

"In the sky," Jackson finished, looking out of the hole next to Carter's. He eyed the cloud wall. "How the heck do we get up there?"

They continued on the path up to the top of the volcano. It, too, was rimmed by lava rock, but everything beyond the rim was covered in snow. Clouds flew by and dumped heavy amounts of snow onto the mountain, never stopping or even slowing along their way. They passed over, circled back, and passed over again in a continuous circle of bombing runs. Meanwhile, darker clouds, flickering with lightning, hovered a safe distance away between the volcano and the cloud wall, an assembled force on alert. As Jackson and Carter climbed out of the volcano, the dark clouds inched closer.

The sky was growing dark. Off in the distance, the sun dragon was sinking below the horizon, its fire dying down as if the day had taken its toll and it had nothing left. The boys knew how it felt. As the world went dark, so did their spirits. All that time and effort, all those challenges, and Campbell wasn't even here. They didn't even know where she was. They could guess she was somewhere up in the sky, somewhere beyond the enormous wall of clouds, but they didn't *know*. They didn't even know how they would get up there to look, or what other challenges they would face once there.

Carter turned to see how far they had come, how far they would have to come *again* if they didn't reach Campbell this time. Off in the distance, the Terra's crystal castle was sparkling with the dragon sun's last light. It looked like someone had dropped a pile of huge orange glowsticks.

Meanwhile, behind his back, the dark clouds crept closer. "Carter," Jackson said. "We've got company!"

Carter turned to see the dark clouds floating toward him, looking more and more like dragons as they approached. *Dragon clouds*, he thought. They had hollow eyes that lit up with each flicker of lightning. "They're surrounding us," Carter said as they spread out in a circle around the top of the volcano.

"What do we do? How do you fight *clouds!?*"

"They're going to spit lightning!" Carter shouted. "We need to find cover!"

Jackson tried to step away, but he couldn't move his feet. Only then did he notice they were buried in the snow. No—not buried. The snow had grabbed hold of his ankles! "I can't move!" he shouted.

Carter rushed to help him, only to have the snow grab him by the legs, too. "I'm stuck, too!"

The dragon clouds drifted closer. They had the boys surrounded, their insides flashing with such intensity, such anger, that their eyes looked afire. One opened its mouth, roared thunder and then spit a bolt of lightning at Jackson. He ducked and the lightning passed over his head.

The ground shook, and the chunk of snow that had Jackson by the feet broke lose and slid down the mountain in a full-blown avalanche.

"Jackson!" Carter shouted as his brother disappeared inside a storm of snow that went charging down the mountainside.

Carter's snow broke free with the rest, but he dove for the volcano's opening and grabbed onto the lava rock. He rose to his feet and scanned the side of the mountain, trying to find his brother. Above, the dragon clouds closed in on him. They shot bolts of lightning at him from all directions. He dodged and weaved and then dove into the volcano with lightning bolts crossing the sky above him.

Carter pushed back against the wall to stay out of sight. He sat down for a moment to catch his breath and think through his next move. There was no making it to the cloud wall with those dragon clouds out there. So his best option now was to go back down the mountain and see if he could find Jackson.

He felt a presence overhead and looked up to see the dragon clouds had closed in on the rim of the volcano. *Are they coming inside?* he wondered. If they did, they'd get him for sure. He side stepped along the wall of the volcano, doing his best to stay out of sight as he made his way back down the path.

The dragon clouds closed in, completely covering the top of the volcano. One shot a lightning bolt at Carter and he dove to the ground to escape it. He popped back up ran as fast as he could down the path.

He was about to reach the lava tube that led out to the cave when the mountain shook and the volcano erupted a jet of hot ashy air, peppered with boulders—and Carter! The eruption blasted through the dragon clouds and sent Carter flying miles into the sky. *Not again!* he thought as he felt the harsh tug of gravity pull him back down toward the ground. He was an instant away from splashing down into the volcano's boiling lava lake, when . . .

***

Carter bolted up, his heart racing, struggling to catch his breath. He felt the presence of his brother's bed next to his, but he didn't want to look at it, afraid of what he would see— or rather, not see. Finally, after his chest had stopped thundering, he spun to his feet and stood before his brother's bed: it was empty. Jackson was gone. He searched the other rooms upstairs, then downstairs. There was no sign of his brother, or Bailey. The house was empty and the silence felt overbearing.

Carter went cold as he considered the situation: he went to save Jackson and Campbell, but lost Bailey instead. He would have to go back *again*. By himself. He thought of the hoodoo dragons, the tiger dragons, the dragon ants, the dragon boulders, the dragon clouds, and who knew what else. He could feel his resolve draining. He needed to eat more dragon fruit *now*, before he lost his nerve. He raced to the kitchen and opened the fridge. To his horror, the dragon fruit was gone.

17

Dragon Campbell

Campbell wasn't sure she could go on walking much longer. It wasn't that her sides or legs ached the way they do when she would run for a long time or walk too far. It was that this part of Atmos was so *boring*. Insufferably boring! She would rather be stuck in the cloud prison or—gasp!— even answering Felton's boring questions than be walking through an endless expanse of clouds where there was nothing to do and even less to see.

The cloud islands around the main island, the one with Airon's mountain, were all densely populated with several other hills and mountains. But out by Felton's lair it was an absolute wasteland. And as she travelled further away, hopping from one island to the next, things grew more and more desolate. The island she was on now was the worst one yet: no mountains or hills—nothing!

She was so bored, she almost didn't realize a dirty little dragon cloud had started trailing behind her. First, she just noticed it felt a little cooler. Then she noticed she was in the shade, a moving shadow encircling her. Only then did she look up to see the small, dark dragon cloud flickering with the threat of lightning. *It's been following me,* she realized.

It was difficult to tell, but she got the sense it was confused and probably wondering what she was doing out here all by herself. The dragon cloud's confusion confused Campbell. Why hadn't it attacked her? Didn't it know who she was?

Better not wait around long enough for it to figure it out, she thought.

She spotted a wispy section of cloud in the ground ahead—*A door!* It was the first thing she had seen for miles. She continued at her current pace until she got nearer and then, without warning, sprinted and dove into the hole and splashed down into an icy lake.

She swam for the surface and shook the water from her eyes. She collected her breath and took in her surroundings: a huge underground lake inside a giant cloud cavern. *Actually, wouldn't that make this an under*cloud *lake,* she wondered. *It is under clouds after all.*

The top of the cavern looked like a patterned quilt made up of light and dark clouds. The light clouds allowed faint rays of sunlight into the cavern, whereas the dark clouds dumped endless showers of rain into the lake.

A ledge continued along the outside of the lake like a walking path. At one end, it widened into a large alcove with a small section of stadium seating facing the water. Directly opposite the alcove, on the other side of the lake, there was a large opening. *Another door!*

Campbell swam to the ledge, climbed out of the lake and raced toward the opening. As she got closer, she heard the sound of rushing water. The lake emptied out of the opening and poured down toward the ground in a seemingly endless waterfall. It dropped so far down she couldn't even hear the sound of the water crashing at the base of the falls.

She turned back to look for another way out when she spotted something in the lake. A dragon! It was just beneath the surface, watching her! It was smaller than the others. It had yellow spiky hair and a snout nose, but less snouty than other dragons. Its hide looked more like skin than scales. It had curious eyes, like it was studying her just as much as she was studying—

And that's when Campbell realized it was her reflection. *She* had yellow spikes for hair! She tried to comb the spikes down with her fingers, but it was no use; they just sprang right back up. The spikey hair wasn't too awful, she kind of looked like Glo from Dance Party. But her nose! What looked less snouty for a dragon was intolerably snouty for a girl! Only her eyes were unchanged.

How much longer do I have before I'm all dragon? she wondered. But she didn't have long to dwell on it—a commotion across the lake commanded her attention. Three Aerials had dropped into the alcove from a door above. They no sooner settled onto the stadium seats when another commotion came splashing its way up the waterfall. Two sea serpents and something that looked like a dolphin dragon crested the falls and swam across the lake to meet the Aerials. It was some sort of meeting.

"Have you brought the prisoner?" the Aerial asked.

The lead merdragon squeaked and moaned its reply. It sounded like an evil dolphin.

"Yes, I have relayed your request to Airon," the Aerial answered. "You shall have more rain for your rivers. Now for your end of the bargain. Let's see the human."

Campbell's heart leapt. *Human?!* But only one? Who did they capture? Carter? Jackson?

There was another commotion outside. A wave made its way up the waterfall, carrying something inside it, but she couldn't see what it was. The wave crested the edge of the waterfall and swept across the lake towards the alcove. It broke on top of the ledge that bordered the lake and then retreated, leaving its prisoner behind, dripping wet. The prisoner stood and shook out its fur.

Bailey?! What the heck is Bailey doing here?!

"What is this?" the Aerial demanded. "This isn't a human," He turned to his partner, confused: "Is it?"

"It was *with* the humans," his partner replied. "Perhaps it's some other Earth creature?"

The lead Aerial turned back to the merdragons. "We cannot bring this to Airon—he's expecting a human."

The dolphin dragon squeaked an angry reply.

"No. The deal was for a human."

As they argued, Campbell snuck closer, being careful to stay in the shadows and out of sight. Even she was unsure what she was looking at it. From afar, she was certain is was her dog, but as she got closer, he started to look as much like a seahorse. "Bailey?" she whispered.

The seahorse dog snapped to. He looked at her with as much confusion as she was looking at him.

She checked the dragons to make sure it was safe; they were fully engrossed in their argument.

"Bailey." She whispered, beckoning him toward her.

He didn't recognize her face, but he did recognize her voice. Still, he hesitated.

"Bailey. Come on!" she whispered more emphatically.

And with that, he sprang toward her and jumped into her arms. Campbell wasted no time. The second she had a hold of him, she leapt into the air and out of the cavern.

She let him down on solid cloud and they raced away, not stopping until they reached the coast of the cloud island. She grabbed Bailey again and, without even thinking, jumped for the next island. It was only after they were already in the air, after they started to sink in the sky, that she considered she might not have enough strength to make the jump with Bailey in her arms. They were about to miss the cloud and fall from the sky when she willed herself to rise. And it worked! She was rising! She was *flying*!

She landed on the cloud island and released Bailey. The excitement of flying seeped away and was replaced by worry. Not only could she jump super high, not only was she strong enough to easily carry Bailey, she could fly now, too? Was she already more dragon than Campbell? How much time did she have left before her transformation would be complete?

She thought of home: of her mother and father, of her brothers—yes, even Carter. She still remembered them. She might have a snouty-nosed dragon face, but she was still Campbell *inside* her head. She still had time!

She took in her surroundings. It was different here. There was no wind, not a single cloud in the sky, no sound. The cloud ground looked dry and dusty; the air felt empty, oppressive. It was like a desert. A cloud desert with no end in sight. A small wisp of cloud rolled by like a tumbleweed.

She willed herself to action: *You've come this far. You can make it!* And with that, she and Bailey marched on.

18

One Last Chance

Carter sat on the couch in the game room. He turned on Dance Party, but he didn't play it. He just let the intro song play over and over again. He didn't even know why he turned it on, perhaps for relief against the cold silence in the house. His heart was heavy, his mind blank. He felt numb. He would never see his brother and sister again. The weight of that realization was crushing. So he let the song play. He didn't know what else to do.

The front door downstairs opened and he heard his Nana's voice. "Now don't forget, those are your Christmas presents. Nana's on a fixed income."

"I know, Nana. Thank you."

That was Jackson's voice. *Jackson?!*

Carter raced downstairs to find his brother and grandma carrying several shopping bags. From the names on the bags, they had been shopping at the local sporting goods store.

"Jackson?!"

"Look who finally decided to get out of bed," Nana said.

Carter waited for his Nana to shuffle away before he asked, "You escaped?! How?"

"The avalanche carried me towards a pile of boulders at the base of the mountain," he said quietly. "I was just about to smash my head into them when I woke up. You weren't in your bed. I was afraid they had captured you." He gave his brother a hug. "Thank goodness, you made it out!"

***

Jackson led Carter into the garage and over to a work bench. On top were three small pots loaded with soil. "I remembered what dad said about keeping the seeds. So, I planted them," Jackson explained. "Just in case."

On a plate next to the pots were the remaining pieces of dragon fruit, now a bit mangled and seedless. Jackson frowned an apology. "Guess I forgot to put them back in the fridge," he said as he ate half the pieces.

Carter ate the rest. After he swallowed, he asked, "What did you get at the store?"

"I have a plan."

***

Carter and Jackson, each dressed in black bodysuits and wearing goggles and headsets, stood at the edge of the cliff overlooking the valley. They stared at the clouds hovering in the distant sky. They had been standing there for close to ten minutes. They knew what they had to do, but the *knowing* didn't make the *doing* any easier.

"What if they don't work. What if we drop straight down to the ground?"

"You can't get scared, Carter. If you get scared you might wake up, and there's no more dragon fruit."

"I'm not scared," Carter said. The expression on his face suggested otherwise.

"Don't worry, the suits will work. Do you remember what it said in the training video?"

Carter nodded. The boys had spent several hours learning maneuvers.

"Then you'll be fine."

"But what if—"

"—What if we try to hike through the valley again and the dragons get us? Or the dragon trees or dragon rocks or

125

dragon waves or who *knows* what else is out there? One jump and we can fly over all of it."

"If they *work*."

"They'll work. This is our best shot to get to Campbell."

The sky was turning a lighter shade of blue. The dragon sun would rise soon, and like an alarm clock, it would wake all of Dragonland.

"We have to go," Jackson said.

"Parachutes!" Carter exclaimed with frustration. "We should have brought parachutes!"

Jackson wondered what else he could say to reassure his little brother, and then it occurred to him there was one way to convince Carter their suits would work. So, he jumped.

What the—?! Carter thought. One moment Jackson was standing by his side and the next he was gone. Without any warning. Carter felt a tinge of betrayal: how could Jackson jump without him? That feeling quickly turned into relief as he watched his brother soar through the air. The flying suit worked!

Carter took a few steps back, ran as fast as he could for the edge and jumped. He spread his arms and legs and the flying suit caught the wind. He arched his back and rose up into the air, soaring toward the cloud wall in the distance. Further on, the sun dragon crested the horizon, lighting the world.

Jackson dipped and soared over and over again, gaining a little altitude each time. Carter did the same. *This is so much easier*! he thought as he scouted the landscape below and counted all the hazards they were skipping. It was like a cheat in a video game.

Of course, two creatures flying through the air would not go unnoticed in Dragonland. The nearest mountain exploded and several fiery volcanic rocks came screaming toward the boys like flaming banshees.

"Head for the volcano," Jackson said.

"Head *for* it?!"

"We need to get higher."

They banked toward the mountain, swerving and swooping their way through the attack; it was like flying through an asteroid field. The rocks had flaming eyes and fiery mouths and their angry screeches filled the sky.

When they reached the edge of the volcano, they banked again and circled it instead of flying directly overhead. "Not yet," Jackson said. He waited until he saw steam and little rocks sputtering out the top. "Now!"

They swooped over the volcano just as it erupted, firing hot gases and flaming boulders into the air. They tucked their arms and legs and let the eruption blast them several hundred yards into the air like rockets. When they felt their upward momentum slow, they spread their arms and legs to catch the air. They were so high up, the volcanoes below looked like a string of ant hills. The tiny volcanoes continued shooting flaming boulders at the boys, but at this height, the banshees' screams sounded more like frustrated whimpers.

While Jackson and Carter were high enough to soar safely over the volcanoes, they were not high enough to top the cloud wall.

"Now what?"

Jackson scanned the wall. He remembered it looked like the dragon had dragged Campbell into the clouds. "There has to be a door somewhere." The wall looked like an endless patchwork of gray and black clouds, but one section stood out. It was light gray. "See that lighter section midway down? Head for that."

As they neared the wall, several dark dragon clouds came out to meet them, flickering with the threat of lightning.

Carter looked up and down so frequently—checking the volcano, then the dragon clouds—he looked like a bobble head. But whereas the volcanoes tried to blast them with everything they had, the dragon clouds kept their lightning holstered.

"Why aren't the dragon clouds attacking us?"

"I don't know, but let's not wait around for them to change their minds. Follow me."

They tucked their arms and dove for the doorway. As they passed over the last volcano, it shot a fury of flaming rocks at them. At the same time, the sky lit up with bolts of lightning. A screaming rock was about to take Carter's head off when a lightning bolt struck and obliterated it. A shower of tiny rock fragments smattered Carter in the face, and one tore a hole in his suit's wing. He began losing altitude.

Jackson ducked his head and looked under his arm. "Carter, you're too low!"

"I have a hole in my wing!"

Jackson flew through the opening in the cloud wall and skidded to a stop.

Carter smacked into the bottom of the doorway with an "Oof" that knocked the air out of him. The impact bent him in half with his legs dangling over the edge. He was sliding off and there was nothing for him to grab onto.

Jackson jumped and grabbed Carter's backpack just before he slipped off the edge. He pulled his brother back up.

The volcano was still shooting flaming rocks at them, but by the time they reached the doorway, the lightning turned them into whimpering little bits that pelted the boys like sand in a windstorm.

"Come on," Jackson said. They hurried away from the opening. The deeper they walked into the cloud tunnel, the darker it got. It was eerily quiet.

"Man," Carter said after he caught his breath, "did you see that bolt of lightning blast that rock right before it took my head off. How lucky was that?"

But Jackson wasn't sure. *Why didn't the clouds attack us?* "It's like they wanted us to make it up here," he said aloud. *They know we're here, so where are they. It's too quiet.*

When they emerged from the tunnel, he got his answer. An entire army of dragons was there waiting for them. At their lead was a mean, vulture-looking dragon.

Carter turned back to the tunnel to see the clouds in the wall drift inward, squeezing the tunnel closed. There was no escape. The boys stood back to back, waiting for the dragons to make a move.

"What are they waiting for?"

As if in answer to Carter's question, a gust of snarling dragon wind came streaming toward them. "Look out for the wind," Jackson said. "When it comes, jump and spread your arms and legs."

The dragon wind swirled around them, and then closed in, trying to trap them within a tornado. Jackson and Carter jumped and kicked out their arms and legs. When the wind caught their flying suits, it whipped them around a few times and then shot them up into the sky. Carter shook his head in a daze; he felt like he had just gotten off the Tea Cups at Disneyworld.

Two dragon winds shot up from the ground after them, but instead of trying to wrap them up in tornados, this time they crashed right into them. But that only shot the boys up higher into the sky. When his ascent stopped, Jackson tucked his arms and legs, did a backflip in the sky to reorient himself, then used the momentum to soar over the dragons. Carter followed his lead.

The dragons didn't chase after them. They just stood there looking stupefied. "The girl spoke true," Vulture said to himself. "They *can* fly." Although he didn't understand how—he didn't see any air plains.

The dragon wind gave chase and quickly caught up to the boys. But this time, they didn't attack. Instead, they flew next to them, their mouths in a snarl, like fighter jets escorting enemy aircraft.

Carter scanned the cloudscape. There were large cloud islands everywhere, spreading out toward the horizon as well as rising up into the sky. But there was no doubt where they needed to go. One giant mountain dominated everything in sight.

"That's got to be where they're holding Campbell," he said.

"Why aren't they trying to stop us." First the dragons let them up here, now they seemed to be escorting them toward the giant cloud mountain, like they wanted them to go there. "It feels like a trap."

As soon as they arrived at the sky moat that surrounded the giant mountain, a dozen dragon winds came at them from all directions, swooping down on them, up from below, trying to grab hold of them, but only tossing them around the sky like pinballs.

There were clouds everywhere—above, below—and Carter didn't know which way was up, which way to fly. A dragon wind shot out and wrapped around his legs like a lasso and tied them together. It flipped him and dragged him off upside down. Behind him, Carter saw Jackson tossing around in the sky like a shirt in the washing machine. But they hadn't captured him yet.

A gust of dragon wind chomped Jackson's foot; another gust grabbed his other leg. It looked like they would tear him in half. Jackson kicked wildly to free himself, then balled up and dropped like he was cannonballing into a pool. He leaned forward into a dive, then spread out to catch the wind again and used his speed to soar upward toward Carter. He grabbed his brother's hands and swung, using his weight and momentum to break Carter free from the dragon wind's grasp. But as he did, another huge dragon wind swallowed him feet first and encircled him in a tornado. He was trapped. He tried to locate his brother, but he couldn't see past the wind swirling around him. "Carter, did you get away?" He shouted into headset.

"No," Carter answered, clearly out of breath. "They get you, too?"

"Yeah."

"So, now what?"

"Save your energy," Jackson said. "I have a feeling we're going to need it."

The two dragon tornadoes carried their prisoners into the giant cloud mountain. The boys couldn't see anything, but they heard a great commotion around them, like they were in the middle of a football stadium, the crowd stomping the seats, cheering the home team, and cursing the visitors.

19

The Edge of the World

Campbell knew the Earth was round and what looked like its edge—the horizon—was just an illusion. You could never reach the end because there was no end. You would just keep going around in a circle. And the horizon would always be off in the distance, unreachable as you travelled around the Earth. But as she and Bailey walked forward, what at first she took for the horizon, looked like an actual end. The end of Dragonland. Whether the world was actually dissolving into nothingness or disappearing into a mist, she couldn't be sure. But everything lost its clarity, its sharpness, little by little until it all just vanished like smoke disappearing into the air.

What happens if we keep going? she wondered. *Will we disappear, too?*

She opened the human diary and flipped through the pages, noting the various drawings: the wall of clouds, Airon's cloud mountain, a landscape with several cloud islands, each with its own cloud mountain rising from the center. She stopped on a drawing that looked like clouds disappearing into a mist. It looked like the scene before her. She wasn't the best reader, didn't know all the words, but there were three words she had no problem reading: "The way home?"

But it was a question, not an answer. She looked up and considered the scene before her. She had seen fog before, but there was always a trace of something beyond the mist. Here, there was only nothingness.

Bailey sniffed, exploratory at first, then with growing excitement.

"What is it Bailey?"

And then, without any warning, he raced into the mist.

"Bailey, wait!"

But he was already gone.

"Bailey?! Bailey come back here!"

She heard him barking, urging her to follow. *Well,* Campbell thought, *whatever happens, it can't be any worse than being an annoying dragon for the rest of my life*

She had no sooner made up her mind to enter the mist when Felton dropped from the sky, right in front of her. His eyes burned accusingly—more hurt than anger. "Hide and seek?" he asked wryly.

Campbell gauged her chances of rushing past him—she was so close! But she opted for another approach: "And you found me! You win!"

"Don't insult me with more deceit. You were trying to escape."

She paused, not sure if she should come clean, when the emotion burst out of her. "Can you blame me, Felton? I miss my home, my family. I want to play Dance Party for *real*, and host *real* tea parties, and grow up and go to prom and get married. I'm a human, I *want* to be a human. Can't you understand that?" She saw the hurt in his eyes, and it quieted her.

He exhaled slowly and a sad smile crept onto his face. "It would have been nice to have someone to play Dance Party with." He sighed. And then he stepped aside.

"Thank you," Campbell started to say when a commotion behind her caught her attention. Thousands of dragons from every cloud in Atmos were taking to the sky, whooping and hollering on their way toward Airon's mountain.

"What's going on?"

"Ah, they must have captured Carter the Smelly Pants," Felton said. "Everyone is going to watch the games."

"What games?"

"The way you told of his skill as a dragon slayer, they want to see him in action. Airon is going to make him fight every Terra prisoner until either he or the Terras are no more."

"You knew about this? Why didn't you tell me?"

"Why, you want to watch?" He looked to the mist as if to add, *But you're almost home?*

"No! We have to stop it!"

"Stop it? Why would you want to do that? You said yourself, he's a monster."

"I never said that!"

"Maybe you didn't use the word 'monster,' but you spoke about him as if he were the most horrible person ever to walk the Earth."

"I did not."

Felton gave her a look that challenged: *Didn't you?*

"I always talk about Carter that way."

And with that, it hit her: she was always badmouthing her brother, was always telling on him and exaggerating to get him in trouble. And yet, Carter *still* played with her. He even played Tea Party with her. He didn't like it and he complained the entire time. But still, he did it. For her. And how did she repay him? By getting him in trouble the moment she didn't get her way.

She felt horrible. She said all those terrible things about Carter without even considering what the dragons might think, what they might do to him. And this time, instead of getting sent to his room, he might—she didn't even want to think it.

The tears came to her voice before her eyes. "I need to go back and help him!"

"Why would he need *your* help? Isn't he supposed to be invincible?"

"Dragonsbane is just a game, Felton. It's not real."

Felton shook his head sadly. "Is nothing you say true?"

"I didn't lie. You just . . . misunderstood."

"You misled me."

"I was just playing. I never thought he might actually get hurt. I have to go back. I have to tell them the truth."

"Why would they believe you?"

"Because . . . well, because it's the *truth*."

"They'll just think it's another one of your tales. You said what you said and there's no unsaying it now. You won't be able to save him. You'll only endanger yourself. This is your last chance to go home. Don't risk it."

Campbell looked into the mist. She imagined her home, her parents, just feet away on the other side. She was so close. And her time was almost out.

20

The Games

When the tornadoes finally unraveled and released them, Jackson and Carter found themselves in the middle of a giant cloud stadium. Dragons dropped in by the hundreds through the rainbow ceiling and took their seats on the upward-spreading rings of clouds that surrounded the inner pit.

At the far end, the largest dragon the boys had even seen sat on his sparkling throne. He waited for the crowd to settle down before he rose to his full height and bellowed with great showmanship, "So, Carter the Smelly Pants, you have come to slay dragons, have you?!"

Carter leaned toward his brother. "Did that dragon just call me a smelly pants?"

"Sounds like they've been talking to Campbell."

Carter rolled his eyes: *Figures.*

Airon continued playing to the crowd: "Well, we don't want to disappoint you! We have assembled some of the fiercest Terras in all of Dragonland for you to fight." He waved his claw in the air, "Let the games begin!"

Dark dragon clouds floated down and formed a ring above the inner pit. They shot constant streams of lightning to create an electrified fence boxing the boys in.

"Oh, great. It's a cage match?!"

The ground rumbled and began to transform. Part of the floor split apart to reveal a small underground lake. A cloud hill rose from its center. Sharp stalagmites shot up from areas around the lake, towering into the air like a giant icy forest; they glowed in the colorful light.

The crowd waited expectantly for the terrain to finish transforming and then cheered the results. They stomped their feet in a repeated pattern: one-two-three. One-two-three. One-two-three. They were calling for a fight.

"This can't be good," Carter said. The boys scanned the terrain to devise a plan. "Can the Terras swim?" Carter asked.

"Not very well. When it gets here, we can dive into the lake and head for the hill. If he comes for us, we can jump off and fly over him to the other side of the lake."

"And how long are we supposed to keep that up?"

"Until he gets too tired to fight, I guess."

"And what happens if *we* get too tired?"

Jackson didn't answer. About fifty feet opposite them, a hole opened in the cloud ground. The crowd began hooting and hollering. The boys readied their paint guns and eyed the hole, wondering what to expect: a bear dragon? Tiger dragon? Something worse.

Something shot out from the hole and landed just a few yards in front of them. Whatever it was, it wasn't a bear or tiger dragon, and it definitely wasn't something worse. Heck, it was smaller than they were.

"*That's* the fiercest Terra in all of Dragonland?" Jackson said in utter confusion.

The crowd was just as confused. The cheering and stomping were interrupted by a thousand voices saying, "Huh?"

Carter aimed his paint gun at the dragon's eyes, but something gave him pause. Whereas the other dragons looked like various animals, this dragon looked . . . *human*. It kind of looked of like—

"Carter, if you shoot me, I swear . . ."

Carter couldn't believe his eyes. Her hair looked more like spikes and there was a definite snout-like quality to her nose and mouth. But he recognized her eyes. *"Campbell?! What did they do to you?"*

"I know, right? So annoying!"

"What are you doing here?!" Jackson asked as she rushed to their side.

"I came to get you out of here. But then you *have* to play Tea Party with me!"

The boys were too stunned to answer.

"Okay?"

"Okay, okay!"

"Come on!" She led them to the hole in the ground just as a dragon tornado blew out past them. As it rose into the sky, the hole closed and then the tornado lowered their real opponent into the ring.

It was the bear dragon. It seemed disoriented at first, unsure what it was supposed to do, a bit unnerved by the large crowd. But then it noticed the boys and smiled a smile that said: *Finally, I get my revenge.*

"The hill!" Jackson shouted, and he and Carter dove into the lake. Campbell flew up to the top of the hill and waited for them.

The bear dragon rushed to the edge of the lake, but paused. It didn't trust the water. It watched as Jackson and Carter pulled themselves onto the island and climbed to the top of its hill. The bear dragon surveyed the terrain, then picked out the largest stalagmite near the water's edge. Using its shoulders, it pushed the stalagmite over like a fallen tree, creating a bridge to the lake's island.

Campbell watched as the bear dragon slowly made its way across, then she jumped down to the water's edge.

"Campbell, what are you doing?"

"Get back up here!"

She burped and a stream of fire shot out at the icy bridge, melting its center enough that it snapped in two. The bear dragon dropped into the water but grabbed hold of the snapped ice stalagmite to help keep itself afloat. It kicked its way over to the island and climbed ashore. It looked toward the boys, then at Campbell, holding the pointy half of the stalagmite like a spear. She was closer.

Campbell read the bear dragon's face. She knew what it was thinking: easier target. She flew up into the air, across the water.

"Campbell, look out."

She turned just in time to see the icy spear flying at her. She flew up higher to dodge it but rose too high and struck the lightning fence. Sparks flew all around her and she collapsed to the ground, unconscious and smoking. The spear crashed into a stalagmite behind her and snapped its top; the sharp tip dangled above Campbell's head, about to fall and impale her at any moment. The bear dragon roared. It leapt across the lake but fell short of the opposite shore and splashed into the water.

Carter swooped down from the hill and pulled his sister out of the way just as the stalagmite tip fell and stabbed the ground. The crowd 'Oohed.' *The human flew!*

Carter brushed the hair out of his sister's face. "Campbell? Campbell are you okay?"

"I got her," Jackson said. He handed his gun to Carter and picked Campbell up in his arms. "When that bear dragon charges, blind him."

Campbell awoke to find Carter, a paint ball gun in each hand, standing guard before her. Jackson caried her behind the broken stalagmite and set her down. The bear dragon clawed its way back onto shore. It shook the water from its face and locked eyes with Carter.

Carter heard his brother grunting behind him, like he was moving something heavy, but he didn't dare take his eyes off the bear dragon to look. "What are you doing?"

"Stand your ground until he lunges for you, then dive out of the way."

Carter nodded, keeping his eyes on the bear dragon. It stalked toward him slowly at first as if it needed time to plan its attack. Then it charged.

"Shoot it!" Jackson shouted, but his little brother just shook his head. "Carter!"

Carter stood his ground, waiting, eying the bear dragon's rear legs for a sign he was about to—

The bear dragon crouched on its haunches and Carter fired at its face with both guns just as it launched into the air. It dodged the first paint pellet only to turn right into the second one. Paint splattered across its snout. Carter continued to fire until every inch of the creature's face was covered in paint. Then he dove out of the way. The bear dragon sailed over him, and Carter heard a tearing sound followed by an angry, pained howl.

Carter rolled over to see Jackson had propped up the felled stalagmite like a spear and its tip pierced the bear dragon through its shoulder. It was still blinded by the paint and had no idea what had happened. It was still alive, but its fight was gone.

There was a long silence as the crowd tried to figure out what had just happened. There was no cheering, no joy in this victory. Airon nodded as if the episode had recalled all sorts of memories. "You see?" he called out to the audience. "It is not the human's size, nor its ferocity that poses a threat, but their trickery." He took a moment to stare Carter down. "Okay, Carter the Smelly Pants. You have proven you can slay a dragon when the odds are in your favor. Let's see how you do with even odds."

The three kids gathered in a line facing the area where the hole had opened up earlier. As they awaited the arrival of their next opponents, Carter turned to his sister: "Campbell, why are they calling me Carter the Smelly Pants?"

"I told them all about you. They think you're worse than Genghis Khan now." Carter stared at her in disbelief. "I may have exaggerated a bit."

"Campbell, can we get out of here through that hole?" Jackson interjected.

"It's how I got in."

"Here, put this on," Jackson said, handing her a headset from his backpack. He inched closer to the hole and the others followed. "He said he was evening the odds, so there's going to be three of them. Wait for the third one to come out, then jump into the hole before it closes."

The tornadoes burst out like cannon fire—boom, boom, boom.

"Now!"

The kids rushed to the hole. Above their heads, three tiger dragons hung in the air. Seeing the kids trying to escape, the dragon tornadoes dropped the tiger dragons from midair. The tiger dragons spread their claws, ready to impale the kids upon landing, but the kids slid underneath them and into the hole just as it closed.

***

After a long dark fall, the kids dropped into an enormous cloud cavern. Jackson spread his arms and legs to catch the air and sailed over to an opening at the far side. Carter followed him.

"No!" Campbell shouted. "Not that way!"

The boys pulled up and dropped to the ground just before the hole. Campbell joined them at the opening, and all three looked out. Dotting the sky below was a long line of cloud cells like the ones from the sky dungeon. Each one carried a Terra prisoner, and they stretched all the way down and across Atmos towards the prison, like a never-ending prisoner transport train. Dragon wind swept along the cloud train like guards keeping tabs on their prisoners.

"What the—!" Carter exclaimed.

"They were going to make you fight all of them," Campbell explained.

"We'll never make it back to the clearing through all that."

"We don't want to go to the clearing." Campbell led the boys toward the opening at the opposite end of the cloud cavern. "We need to cross the mist at the far edge of Atmos. That's the way home." They reached the other opening and looked out. "You see where everything just disappears?"

"You mean the horizon?"

"That's the mist." She handed the journal to Jackson, opened to the drawing of the mist with the words, "the way home."

"Like your dream," Jackson said to Carter.

"We have to go save Bailey first!" Carter replied. "You promised."

"He already went home," Campbell said.

"You saw him?" Jackson asked. "But the Mers had him."

"They were trading him to the Aerials when I found him and helped him escape."

"Why didn't you go with him?" Carter asked.

"I heard you were captured," she said with a shrug. "You're my brothers. I have to look out for you."

Carter gave her shoulder an affectionate squeeze, his way of saying thank you.

Jackson smiled, then turned to survey the sky outside. "I don't see any dragons out there yet, but you can bet they're going to come after us."

"It's so far," Carter said, his hope fading. "You sure we can make it with all the dragon clouds and dragon wind—not to mention the *dragons*—chasing us."

Just then the sound of a hurricane being shot out of a cannon came crashing down from the tunnel above.

"Well, we can't stay here!"

"Follow me!" Campbell shouted before diving out into the sky.

The boys followed just as the cavern erupted into a frenzy of wind and thunder and the roar of dragons echoing off the walls. And then a boom rang out as every cloud in the sky, every gust of wind, every Aerial came shooting out of the mountain after them.

"I'm losing altitude." Carter said into his headset.

"Me too. I think our flying suits are too wet." They were falling too fast to clear the cloud island below. "We can't land on that cloud. We might be able to outfly them, but we'll never outrun them."

"I'm not going to make it."

Campbell swept around and above them. *I was strong enough to carry Bailey*, she thought. "Get closer together," she shouted. They did, and she grabbed each of their backpacks in her claws and dragged them past the island and across the sky.

Jackson heard the full fury of Atmos closing in on them. He looked back at their pursuers. "They're gaining on us. Campbell, just leave us! You can still make it out of here."

"I'm not leaving you!"

Carter looked down to make sure they were over empty sky. "It's okay, Campbell," Carter said. "We don't need to reach the mist. If we fall, we'll wake up before we hit ground."

"Will that work for me?" Campbell asked as she flapped her wings. "What if I'm too much of a dragon to fall?! What if you escape but they catch me before I reach the mist?"

"We need to scare you awake. What are you afraid of?"

"I'm not afraid of anything."

Carter rolled his eyes. *Figures that's what she'd say.*

Jackson looked back at the dragons in pursuit. Vulture was in the lead smiling, confident that in a few more seconds he'd have them. "Campbell, we're running out of time!" he shouted.

Then Carter's face brightened. *"Campbell . . ."*

"What?!"

"While you were gone, I played *Dance Party.* As *Glo.*"

"No, you didn't."

"Yes, I did. *And* I set a new high score."

"Cart—!" but she never finished her scream. In a poof, she was gone and the boys were tumbling through the sky, racing for the ground one moment, and ...

***

. . . Back in their room the next. Carter bolted up and—to his great relief—he saw Jackson awake in bed and his sister on the floor by their beds. His relief did not last long, though. It took Campbell a moment to gather her bearings and realize what had happened before she turned on him. "Carter, how could you?! I'm going to . . . " but her voice faded away before she finished the sentence.

"You're going to what? Tell mom?"

"No." She wrinkled her nose with determination. "I'm going to beat your score!"

And with that, she popped to her feet and headed to the game room. Carter was dumbfounded. He didn't know what to think.

He heard Bailey barking excitedly and could imagine his dog jumping up and greeting Campbell. Then he heard his mother shout: "Campbell!" There was a moment of silence followed by the sound of what Carter assumed were hugs and kisses before his mother continued. "Where have you been?! I heard you scream. What happened?! What did Carter do?"

Carter braced himself for Campbell's answer.

"He helped me get home."

Some Months Later

"Do you want more tea, Carter," Campbell asked.

"Sure," he answered.

She poured more empty air into his cup. "And how about you, Felton?"

They were sitting in her bedroom, her stuffed dragon on one chair, Carter on another, and Felton on the fourth. But rather than answer, Felton grew and transformed until he had turned into Airon.

"Enough of your games, human," Airon bellowed. "Tell me: where is the sacred fruit?"

"I dunno," Campbell said in her most innocent voice.

"Enough of your lies!" Airon shouted, his mouth glowing with the threat of deadly fire.

"Oh my gosh, you're totally ruining our tea party!"

Airon roared and vomited a stream of fire. Campbell felt the heat and . . .

***

Then she woke up. Campbell had been having the same nightmare for weeks. But she no longer woke up screaming from her bad dreams, and she assumed that was because she had become braver after her adventures in Dragonland and learned to conquer her fears, even when asleep. Still, there was something different about this dream, like it was trying to tell her something. That night, she got her answer.

She was watching television with her family when their show was interrupted with "breaking news." There had been another dragon sighting. There had been dragon sightings all over the world for the past few weeks, but they weren't attacking people, at least not yet. They were burning crops.

This time a man had used his phone to shoot video of the alleged dragon. His short video played on the television in a loop.

"I guess it kind of looks like a dragon," her father said.

"Oh please," her mother said. "That could be anything."

But Campbell's heart stopped cold and a chill washed over her. Blurry video or not, she recognized the dragon: it was Vulture. The dragons must have reopened the mist and returned to Earth. And there was no mystery why. Campbell's dreams had been warning her. They were here for the dragon fruit.

She shared a look with her brothers who seemed to be thinking the same thing. They turned and looked out the window at the planter on their back patio where Jackson had planted the three dragon fruit trees. A dozen fruits were growing on their branches. Should they destroy the trees before the dragons find out and come for them? Or will they need the dragon fruit to return to Dragonland? They didn't know the answer. But one thing was clear: their adventures with the dragons were far from over.

About the Author

Michael Eidam has worked in television comedy, journalism, and corporate communications, but his passion has always been to spin a good yarn. He has written three middle-grade novellas: the whimsical allegory *A Delightful Bit of Nonsense* (2024), and the humorous fantasy action-adventure stories *Nightmare in Dragonland* (2023) and *Escape from Sjór Borg* (2018)—the latter written as a promise to his nieces and nephews. His first novel, *Medicine for Mankind* (2016), satirized a power grab following a global pandemic long before Covid showed us how absurd things could get. Ever restless, Eidam has lived in all four corners of the U.S. and its middle. He's even lived a motorhome for a year, touring the western national parks and trekking across Europe. He currently lives in the space between his ears.

www.ingramcontent.com/pod-product-compliance
Lightning Source LLC
Chambersburg PA
CBHW020359130626
46549CB00006B/2345

9 7 9 8 9 8 8 7 3 1 9 0 0